VIRGO INCOGNITO

ZODIAC GUARDIANS 5

TAMAR SLOAN

TRICIA BARR

1

ADA

Ada grips the locket hanging by a chain around her neck as she stares intently at the laptop screen. "Come on, come on," she says under her breath.

"Maybe you chose too big a target."

Ada turns to Eric, arching a haughty brow at him. "Are you doubting me?"

He instantly throws his hands up in surrender, his handsome face all innocence. "I would never," he says, lips twitching.

Ada feels her own mouth wanting to smile, but she represses it. She leans over from the passenger seat of the parked car they're in, pointing a finger at him. "Are you sure? It certainly sounded like it."

Eric's eyes widen in mock horror as he glances at the tip of the finger now an inch from his nose. "I swear! The great Dyad could break any code!"

"Correct answer."

Ada dissolves into giggles as she climbs over a little more, her hand resting on his chest as she presses her lips to his. Although she meant for it to be little more than a caress, the usual electricity sizzles at their touch, familiar and yet exhilarating each and every time.

Eric clasps her face and draws her closer, deepening the kiss. Ada's hands clench in her lap, wanting to grasp him right back, but she keeps them tightly fisted. She almost hurt him last time she did that.

Instead, she pushes forward, intensifying the pressure. She shows Eric with her mouth and lips and tongue how much he rocks her world. No. That he *is* her world.

Eric gasps, leaning in closer. "Ada," he moans.

She draws in a sharp breath at the sound of her name. It's heavy with desire. And yet it soars with love. And Ada's right there with him. She shifts, wishing they were closer, her every cell buzzing with passion. In fact, the air is crackling with its manifestation—electricity.

They draw apart, looking sheepishly at each other. "Sorry," Eric murmurs.

Ada ignores the familiar frustration that's stomping its foot, demanding to be acknowledged. "Never apologize, okay? This isn't on you."

Eric's hands tighten fiercely. "I love you, Ada. I wouldn't have you any other way."

Now that the emotion has dialed down, Ada finally brings her hand up to caress his cheek, soft stubble tickling her fingers. Eric's wintergreen eyes are pools of truth as his gaze doesn't let her go.

"I love you, too," she whispers.

Which is what makes this so hard. Her heart and soul belong to Eric. But her body never will. Not when she's a walking livewire who can't control herself.

The laptop *dings*, and she reluctantly withdraws to her side of the car. "And the results are in."

She scans the screen, reading the messages as they appear. She types a quick response.

"Well?" Eric asks. "Did it work?"

Ada taps the edge of the keyboard impatiently. "We're about to find out."

There's another soft *ding*, and she changes tabs to her offshore bank account. She whoops with jubilation when she sees the balance multiply.

"You did it?" Eric exclaims.

Ada turns to him, grinning so hard it hurts. "*We* did it!"

She may be the front of Dyad, but Ada knows she's nothing without Eric. From the moment they ran away from the group home they were in, she swore she'd find a way to support their life off the radar.

Hacking is what allows her to come good on her promise.

"Oh yeah, baby!" Eric shouts. "Taco Bell, here we come!"

Ada laughs. Eric's love of Mexican food means they always celebrate at Taco Bell. She whoops again, excited that their freedom has once again been secured.

The sounds of police sirens have them both freezing. They spin in their seats, and Ada's heart drops to somewhere near her feet. Two cop cars are roaring down the road toward them.

"The buttheads tracked me?" Ada asks incredulously.

Eric turns the keys in the ignition and slams down the gas. He pulls into traffic, quickly accelerating as he continuously glances in the rearview mirror. "Maybe they're not after us."

Ada holds her breath as she watches over her shoulder. The flashing lights become brighter and the wailing of the siren grows louder as the police cars approach. They split up, moving into a lane on either side of the one she and Eric are driving in.

Then, they accelerate.

Ada spins to face the front as she grips the seat. "Nope, they're after us."

Eric's hands grip the steering wheel as his gaze focuses on the road. "First set of traffic lights is up ahead."

Ada nods, typing rapidly on her laptop. "Got it."

"It's red, Ada," he says tensely.

"I'm on it," she assures him, still typing. "Bingo!"

The lights turn green and Eric accelerates some more. Adrenaline spikes through Ada's veins, fueled both by fear and exhilaration. She uses it to type even faster. "Let me know when."

The roar of the car's engine increases as Eric powers toward the intersection. Ada's finger hovers over the keyboard. It's all in the timing.

The car bottoms out as they hit a dip. "Now!" Eric shouts.

Ada presses the key a moment before they fly through the intersection. The green light instantly turns orange. Behind them, the police cars seem to accelerate.

Ada holds her breath as she waits to see what they're going to do. "Don't risk it," she says under her breath. "It's not worth it."

First one police car, then the second, abruptly brakes, screeching to a halt at the intersection. A moment later, a large truck rumbles past them, blocking Ada's view. She flops back into her seat, letting out the air trapped in her lungs.

"That was close," Eric mutters as he turns down a nearby street.

"Which is what makes it fun," Ada points out.

Eric shakes his head. "Maybe you shouldn't have targeted Sinclair Holdings."

"Pft," she scoffs. "If a simple MITM attack could get me that data, they should be thanking me."

When Ada hacked into their Wi-Fi using little more than a penetration testing app, allowing her to crack passwords and download data, she pointed out their system's vulnerability.

And then all she did was sell back said data. Each time she does this, the companies she targets get to learn where they need to strengthen their systems, she gets paid. Everyone wins.

Ada sets about wiping everything on her computer. "It's a pity, I was getting attached to Cocoa," she says, stroking the hard edge of the screen. She always names her computers, even if she doesn't intend on keeping them.

"As much as Esther?" Eric teases.

"No, definitely not." Ada grins. "Esther is special."

With a flourish, she presses the final key and the screen goes black. "Pull over here."

Eric does as she asks, and Ada quickly hops out and throws Cocoa into a dumpster. "Thank you," she calls as the laptop hits the bottom with a *clang*.

Climbing back in, Ada sighs. "One more thing to do."

Eric nods, his lips tight and Ada hides her wince at his expression. All the moving around is harder for him. To be honest, she was kind of hoping to stay a little longer at their latest place, too.

She ruffles his blond hair, trying to lighten the mood. "You never liked the décor in this place, anyway."

He throws her a rueful glance. "The graffiti clashed with the mold stains."

Ada smiles, glad his usual steady self is back. Eric is her foundation, her earthing rod. If he's okay, then she is, too.

There are no more signs of the police as they make their way back to their latest hangout, but Ada listens in on their comms using her scanner app, just in case. It means they both hear when a frustrated woman calls in that they lost their mark as they pull up beside a dingy abandoned building.

Ada skips out of the car, grinning. She meets Eric at his door and they high five. She presses a quick kiss on his lips just for good measure. They won't need money for several weeks now.

Inside, they make their way around old mattresses and drug paraphernalia to the back corner. This is where their base has been for the past few weeks. There isn't much to pack up. A few clothes shoved in a garbage bag, their sleeping bags and blankets into another. Ada goes to the battered wardrobe in the corner of the room and squats beside it. Pulling away a panel at the base, she slips out her one valued possession.

Esther.

She was the very first laptop Ada bought with her very first hacking payout. With biometric protection, vault-level encryption, a fingerprint sensor integrated into the power button, and military grade standards used in the specs, Esther's powerful but also secure. Apart from Eric, she's the only other soul on this Earth that Ada trusts.

Eric looks around, hoisting the two garbage bags that carry all their possessions. "That's everything. We'd better get going."

Ada sits on a nearby chair, its plastic seat full of small holes the size of a cigarette burn. "I just want to check everything's okay."

Eric rolls his eyes. "I doubt she got up to too much while we were gone." But he puts down the garbage bags he was holding, knowing Ada needs to do this.

She opens Esther and her screen comes to life. "It's not her I'm worried about," she mutters, glancing around the empty building. The transient population that comes and goes are the ones who can't be trusted.

Ada's about to do the usual scans that will tell her if anyone has as much as touched Esther when a box flashes on the screen, making her reel back.

Eric moves around behind her, instantly concerned. "What? What is it?"

Ada points to the words flashing on the screen.

Red code alert.

"It's an alert I've programmed in," she explains, unsure if she's excited or nervous.

"For what?" Eric asks, his voice suddenly cautious.

Ada swallows. "For the FBI."

2

TRISTAN

"Have you found anything?" Jareth asks Tristan as he flops onto a chair beside him.

Tristan groans as he sags in his own chair, turning away from the computer screen. He's spent hours in HQ staring at the thing and it's gotten him nowhere. "I don't even know why I'm trying. If the FBI can't crack this code, then I sure as pitch won't be able to."

Jareth chomps down on his banana. "The code probably wasn't even created in this galaxy," he points out.

"I know," Tristan says on another groan. "Which is why I called the meeting."

As if on cue, Veronica trips down the stairs, looking fresh and bright after a shower. She's been staying the night more and more regularly. She slides onto Jareth's lap, her cheeks turning a cheeky shade of pink. "Hey, there," she purrs.

Tristan turns away, not wanting to begrudge the obvious connection they have. It's not their fault he missed the boat with Brielle. Nor do they need to know how much that knowledge hurts.

Cassandra enters next, Logan with her. Tristan pulls up a

smile during the rounds of hellos, ignoring the way the two hold hands as if they never intend on letting go. It seems like everyone around him has found that one person who makes everything right in their world, no matter how wrong things are.

Everyone except for him.

As if on cue, Brielle appears at the bottom of the stairs. Her coffee-colored hair brushes her shoulders as she scans the room, looking like she's holding her breath. The moment her gaze falls on Tristan, it instantly flickers away.

Tristan keeps his smile in place by locking his jaw. Friends, he tells himself. It's best for everyone.

"Hey," he says warmly. "Last but not least."

As he says it, Tristan realizes she always used to be the first. It usually afforded them a few moments alone together before the others arrived. It seems returning to best friend status is going to be as challenging as he thought it would be.

Brielle nods, her gaze never quite meeting his as she moves to stand beside Cassandra. "Sorry, I baked some white choc and macadamia cookies and they took a couple of extra minutes in the oven," she says, lifting the plastic container Tristan didn't notice her holding.

"Have we told you how much we love you?" Jareth asks, his joy evident.

Brielle flushes, her gaze darting to Tristan and then away again. "You mention it every time I bake," she teases fondly.

Tristan wonders if his teeth are going to fuse together, it's taking that much effort and pressure to keep his smile in place. Those words are ones he can't say.

Because he was too late.

Logan takes the container and opens it, drawing in a deep breath. "He's right, though. You speak the universal language of male love."

Cassandra leans over beside him, her face melting at the

smell. "And if I didn't love you for it as well, then I'd be worried about my man."

Brielle giggles and the others laugh as they pass the cookies around. Tristan almost doesn't take one, feeling a little like he doesn't deserve to, but he knows it will draw attention.

Plus, holy pitch, do they smell good!

Clutching the moist cookie, he clears his throat. "Now that we're all here and sugared up, we need to talk."

Five expectant faces turn toward him and he wishes he had better news.

"I haven't been able to make heads or tails of the code we were given."

No one looks surprised as Logan nods. "The FBI haven't made any headway, either."

"And we need to crack it before they do," Tristan adds.

Jareth scratches his chin. "Any ideas?"

"Actually, I have one," says Tristan. "Zarius used to know a guy who's great with tech. An underground hacker type. I think we should try to find him."

"Do you have any leads on him?" Cassandra asks.

Tristan grins. "I know his name is Klaus."

"I suppose that's something," she says dryly. "I can't help, though. I have some…stuff to deal with at home." She glances at Brielle. "I was hoping you'd come with me?"

Brielle's face brightens just a few too many shades. "Sure."

Although Tristan wonders what just passed between the two girls, he's relieved that Brielle has something to do. Something that doesn't involve being by his side for long periods of time.

It's going to take time to find some sort of equilibrium around her.

"And I'm going to keep an eye on Nebula," says Logan. "If Dad finds anything out, we'll be the first to know."

Tristan nods, conscious of the price Logan is paying to be a Zodiac—betraying his own father.

Veronica claps her hands. "And Jareth should come with you!"

Jareth's eyebrows disappear into his bangs. "He should?"

"Yes." Veronica smiles as she pats his chest. "You Zodiacs should stick together. What if something happened to my brother?"

Tristan suppresses a smile. Veronica is trying to get her brother and boyfriend to spend some time together in her usual completely unsubtle way.

Logan looks at his sister as if she just grew a unicorn horn. "Jareth can't come into the Nebula offices. Dad knows who he is."

"He'll disguise himself with his powers," Veronica responds, rolling her eyes. Logan goes to speak again but she cuts him off. "And if anyone gets suspicious, dial the emotion down using *your* powers and make a hasty retreat."

Tristan can't help himself. "She makes a good argument, boys."

Logan and Jareth's faces mold into the same look of consternation. They glance at each other, obviously unsure of how they've found themselves in this position.

"Excellent," Veronica announces. "It's decided." She spins to face Tristan. "And that leaves me to come with you."

Tristan blinks. He's never worked with Veronica before, not just the two of them. "I suppose it does."

She skips over to stand beside him. "Klaus doesn't stand a chance."

Jareth chuckles as he walks past, Logan doing the same as they both head for the door.

"She's right, he doesn't," calls Jareth over his shoulder.

"Good luck," adds Logan.

Cassandra rushes to catch up with them. "Hang on, I didn't get my goodbye kiss!"

"I hope she's talking to you, Logan," Tristan calls after her.

Brielle heads to the stairs, too. "I'll see you around," she says quietly.

Tristan's heart twinges, like someone just tugged at its very core. "Sure." He hesitates, but then decides to say what's on his mind. "Keep me posted, okay?"

No matter what's going on between them right now, he still needs to know she's safe.

Brielle nods, biting her lip as she turns away. The moment she's gone, Tristan sags against the desk. It's as if she just took his light with him.

"So?" Veronica asks as she spins to face him, her hands hiking to her hips. "What's going on with you and Brielle?"

Tristan scowls. Working with Veronica suddenly feels like a bad idea. "I don't want to talk about it."

"I didn't ask how you felt about the conversation," she retorts, rolling her eyes. "One moment you and Brielle are like two strands of rope—inseparable, and now you're..."

"Friends." Tristan spits the word out like it tastes as unpalatable as it sounds.

"Ah, didn't you two try that? It ended up at its inevitable conclusion—you two locking lips."

Tristan pushes away from the desk he was leaning against. "It's not that simple, Vee."

No matter how much he wishes it was.

Veronica grabs the cookie he's still holding and takes a big bite. "You have a chance at love, you grab it," she says around her mouthful of white choc macadamia. "It really is that simple."

Striding to the stairs, Tristan jams his hands in his pockets. "Can we focus on finding Klaus, please?"

Veronica wrinkles her nose as she sashays past him. "Sure can, Zodiac Leader," she says, saluting him.

Tristan shakes his head, glad she's let the topic go.

Veronica jogs up the stairs, calling over her shoulder. "Although you should know, I'm a very good multitasker."

Tristan groans internally, pushing himself off the wall to follow her. Why doesn't anyone realize his role is to protect the Universe?

And it seems he can't have that and love, too.

3

BRIELLE

"There's no way he's going to be there," Cassandra says as they head to downtown New York City.

"But we have to try," Brielle says, the eternal optimist.

Things were the epitome of awkward between her and Tristan at the meeting, and she has to do absolutely everything to get her mind off it. Part of her—a big part—the biggest part—wants to beg him to forgive her for her mental breakdown and take her back and have them go back to casually dating. But after she accidentally let slip those three most powerful words…and he didn't say them back… There's no recovering from that. Tristan doesn't love her—*can't* love her.

She's not the type to fool around with no strings. That's why she's never dated in her entire life. Not that she has anything against people who do have fun, like Cassandra before Logan, but Brielle needs a deeper commitment than that. And she can't make an exception for Tristan, no matter how phenomenal he makes her feel when he looks at her, holds her hand, kisses her…

Stop it, you masochist!

She has a mission. Find Solomon and the mysterious box he stole.

"Here we are," Cassandra says as they pull up in the parking lot Google Maps directed them to. It's a small yet posh building in the heart of New York City. Brielle could easily see someone like Solomon practicing law here.

"Let's check it out," she says, opening her car door.

They both get out and head to the main entrance. Despite a sign on the door saying "For Lease", Brielle tries the handle. Locked.

"Told ya," Cassandra says impatiently.

"Crap," Brielle mutters.

"Now what?" Cassandra puts her hands on her hips in typical Cassandra fashion.

"Now we investigate our next best lead," Brielle states, heading back to the Mercedes.

"Which is?"

Brielle gives Cassandra a sidelong glance. "Your dad."

Cassandra stiffens, alarm hardening her features for a split second before her face molds into a cool mask. "He hardly makes eye contact with me, let alone speaks to me. I don't think he'll be much help." She looks away, but Brielle can see the pain in those amber eyes.

Brielle chews on her bottom lip for a moment, pondering both the Solomon debacle and the Cassandra-daddy issue. Then she gets an idea. "Well, how about I talk to him?"

Cassandra looks at her sideways, arching a perfectly plucked golden eyebrow.

"Look, we know that he's got a mysterious interest in me," Brielle explains. "He's always asking me to come work for him and weird stuff like that. What if I go to his office pretending to be interested?"

Cassandra's brow pinches with doubt. "And how are you

going to bring up the topic of Solomon? He doesn't know
that we know he hired him to bail you out."

"I'll casually bring up my experience with Solomon at the
courthouse and ask if he's ever dealt with him," Brielle
responds, grasping at straws.

Cassandra scoffs. "Ha! You, casual?" She laughs teasingly,
although Brielle can admit she's not the best at play acting.
"Besides, even if you could bring it up without sounding
suspicious, my dad is way too crafty to fall for any traps.
There's no way he'd give away any important information.
I'm sure at this point he knows the FBI is after Solomon."

Brielle frowns, then sighs. "Well, he's our only connection
to Solomon. We have no other leads to pursue. We have to at
least try."

Cassandra purses her lips in consideration. Suddenly, she
points her index finger in the air, smiling wide. "I just had an
idea!"

Twenty minutes later, they're outside Cassandra's dad's
towering office building.

"How do you know he won't be there?" Brielle asks as
they enter the lobby and head for the elevator. A nervous
knot is forming in her belly.

Cassandra flicks her hair over her shoulder and presses
the *up* button. "My dad's a creature of habit, and he never
deviates from his routine." The doors slide open and they get
inside. Cassandra presses the *ten* button. "Every day between
noon and one, he goes to the same sushi restaurant for lunch,
unless he's entertaining a client, in which case he takes them
to a ritzy Thai place. Trust me, he won't be there."

Brielle gulps as the elevator rises, and her heart jumps

into her throat when the doors open on the tenth floor and they have to step out.

Straightening her shoulders and plastering on that charming smile of hers, Cassandra walks into the lobby like she owns the place, and Brielle has no choice but to follow. They go up to the front desk where a very beautiful woman with short blonde hair and heavily lined eyes types away at her laptop. She looks like a supermodel, and Brielle's feelings of intimidation skyrocket to the point she has to clench her fists to not turn around.

Cassandra folds her arms on the desk and playfully leans forward. "Hi, Jeanie!" she greets chipperly. "Is my dad in?"

The gorgeous Jeanie raises her stunning dark eyes to regard them. "Sorry, Hun, he went out to lunch." She glances at the wall hung with various clocks timed to countries all around the world. "Shouldn't you be in school, young lady?"

"Actually, it's fall break," Cassandra says with a shrug. "But I have a paper to write for econ due when we return, and I think my textbook got mixed up with Dad's work stuff over the weekend—I can't find it anywhere and I'm freaking out!" Her pitch heightens at the end with her faux dismay.

Brielle ignores the lie detection alarms going off in her head and focuses on how impressed she is with Cassandra's easy ability to lie on command, and to do it so convincingly.

"I came down here hoping to catch him before he left," Cassandra continues. "Can you please let us in so we can look for it?" She widens her puppy dog eyes to amp up her plea. When Jeanie glances at her laptop skeptically, Cassandra adds an imploring pout.

"Oh, alright," Jeanie concedes with a sigh, then rises from her desk and fiddles with a set of keys. "But be quick about it."

"Of course," Cassandra says, happily skipping after Jeanie

toward the door with shiny gold letters that read Richard Sinclair, SFO.

Jeanie unlocks the door and ushers them inside. When she doesn't immediately leave them to it, Cassandra makes a show of looking for the fictitious textbook on the desk. She and Brielle share a glance that says, "What are we going to do now?"

Luckily, the front desk phone rings, and Jeanie has to answer it. Dropping her shoulders in relief, Cassandra rushes to close the door and lock it, giving them at least some warning before the secretary returns.

"Okay, we don't have long," Cassandra says in a hushed tone as she scurries to the filing cabinet and opens a drawer. "My dad is notoriously thorough and keeps huge files on every single person he works with. He even runs background checks on delivery runners before he hires them to carry packages across town. I'm sure he'll have one on Solomon."

Brielle opens a drawer too, rifling through folders even though she has no idea what she's looking for. "And how do you know he doesn't keep that stuff digital?"

"He doesn't trust electronic information, mostly because he knows exactly how to steal information that way from other people," Cassandra explains, her face practically buried in the drawers she's searching. "He always keeps the important stuff in hard copy."

Brielle nods and focuses on the task at hand. She reads each name one by one at the top of each folder. There's no clear order to them, certainly not alphabetical. And if there's any other categorization for the folders, it's not labeled.

"How does your dad find anything in all this mess?"

"He groups people by how important they are, whether they're clients or employees, independent contractors, persons of interest," Cassandra lists.

"Why doesn't he label them as such?" Brielle complains,

flipping from Barnes, C. to Milner, A. to Jacobs, T. She's never going to find Gray, S. in all this chaos.

"For this exact reason," Cassandra says with a short chuckle. "The only thing my dad trusts is that he can't trust anyone. Turns out he's right. Ah!"

"What?" Brielle springs up in alarm.

"Found it!" Cassandra yanks out a file and opens it on the desk.

They both hunch over it, devouring it with intense scrutiny. Inside is a background check printout listing all of Solomon's pertinent information like birthdate, place of birth, social security number, as well as his history like his educational institutions, GPA throughout, former addresses, past employers—even his first job at Dairy Queen—everything. His entire life is summed up on these few pages.

Including his current address.

"We need to make a copy of this," Brielle whispers.

"No time." Cassandra whips out her phone and begins snapping a picture of each page.

The loud clacking of heels from outside the door alerts them that Jeanie is off the phone.

And on the move!

Cassandra snaps one last picture, then closes the folder and shoves it back into the cabinet. Brielle hopes she put it back where it was, but there's no time to ask. Cassandra pushes the drawer closed as quietly as she can as they hear the jingle of keys and the lock being turned.

Jeanie opens the door, and Cassandra feigns frustration, pretending to search.

Cassandra throws up her hands. "Well, I just can't find it." She grunts for show, then heads for the door. "Thanks anyway, Jeanie. I guess I'll just have to wing it for the test."

"Okay..." Jeanie seems at a loss as Cassandra and Brielle pass her. "Good luck."

"Thanks," Cassandra calls without looking back, then steps into the elevator just as a couple of suited men exit.

The doors slide closed and the elevator begins its descent, and Brielle lets out a heavy breath, her heart pounding. She's really not cut out for espionage, and she's glad Cassandra did all the talking—and lying.

"Now we go to this address and see if he's skipped town yet," Cassandra says.

Brielle nods.

The sudden buzzing of her phone makes her jump, then she relaxes as she realizes it's just that. She pulls it out. It's a text from Frank.

Her heart gallops with renewed speed as she fears he's found out she's not in school. After the recent FBI situation, she doesn't want to give him more to worry about.

She opens the message. *"Come home right after school. We need to talk."*

4

CASSANDRA

Another dead end.

Cassandra sinks into the driver's seat of her Mercedes, letting out a heavy sigh. She'd gone to the address listed as current on Solomon's rap sheet, a posh apartment on the upper east side, and the next door neighbor informed her that he'd moved out in the middle of the night.

Of course, Cassandra had expected as much. If her dad had been able to find Solomon's address, so could the FBI. Solomon would have known he'd have to run.

She had just hoped she'd beat him to it.

Now she sits alone in her car, wondering what to do. She dropped Brielle off right after they'd left her dad's office. She wishes Brielle hadn't needed to go home. Now Cassandra has no one to bounce ideas off of. All she has is a few pictures in her phone of Solomon's life story, and not a single thing in any of that text gives her a clue where to look next.

Everyone else has a task. Her boyfriend is off with Jareth investigating Nebula, and Tristan and Veronica are trying to crack some apparently vital code. Her job, finding Solomon and the mysterious ancient box he stole, is perhaps the most important one.

And she's failing at it.

She shuts off her phone's screen and drops it into the cupholder in the center console, then starts her car. Even if she doesn't know what to do with the info on the background check, Logan probably will. She'll wait for him to return from his stakeout and meet up to see what they can find together.

Until then, she has no other choice but to go home. And lately, it hasn't felt like much of a home. Her dad avoids her at all costs and her mom acts like she's invisible. How did things get like this? Her mom used to at least pretend to love her. As for her dad… Sometimes, when the house is at its most silent, her mind whispers a thought she won't let herself form into words: Is no attention really better than negative attention?

She shakes her head, inviting thoughts of Logan to distract her as she drives. That definitely does the trick. It's only a couple minutes before her cheeks burn and her lips spread. Logan is just as delicious as his chocolate eyes promise, and she's so happy that things worked out between them. She can hardly wait to see him later.

When she pulls up into her driveway, she notices that both her mom's and dad's vehicles are also parked there. She looks at the clock on her dash. It's only three o'clock, an unusually early time for her dad to be home, especially since her rebellion.

A sinking feeling weighs her gut down as she exits her car and walks to the front door. She turns the knob and enters. Both her parents are sitting at the kitchen table, looking at her with grave expressions on their faces.

"What did you take, Cassandra?" her father accuses before the door closes behind her.

"W-what?" she stammers. Even after several days of him not speaking to her, his angry and authoritative tone is just as frightening as before, and she feels again like the cowering little girl at his mercy.

He crosses his arms over his chest and narrows his eyes into slits. "You were snooping around my office today. So I'll ask you one more time, what did you take?" He says each word very slowly, making her feel even more like a child being reprimanded.

She hates it. She hates him for making her feel this way. She hates herself for letting him continue to have this power over her.

Cassandra promised herself when she became a Zodiac Guardian that she would never bow to his will again, and she's not about to break that promise now.

She summons her courage and straightens her spine. "I didn't take anything. I was just looking for a textbook I thought you might have taken to work by mistake."

He slams his fist on the table, and it takes everything she has not to flinch. "Jeanie may have bought that crap, but I know better. You were snooping in my office, and I demand to know what you were looking for."

"After everything we've done for you," her mom chides, venom in her green eyes. "We brought you into our home and treated you like our very own daughter. We raised you, cared for you, gave you everything you could ever want or need. And you repay us by first lying that your father hurts you, and now stealing from him." She shakes her head, and the contempt on her face slices through Cassandra's chest like a white hot knife.

A smug smirk twitches at the corner of her dad's mouth at his wife's defense of him.

As usually happens, the hurt turns into anger. "I'm not lying, and you both know it." Cassandra locks eyes with her mom. "You're just too afraid to admit to yourself that you married a soulless monster."

"I want you out of this house."

Her dad's booming declaration bounces off the white walls and floor of the kitchen, coming at her in stereo.

For a moment, Cassandra's too stunned to speak. *Did he really just say that?*

"What?" she asks, her voice suddenly sounding small.

"You're no longer welcome under our roof," her mom rephrases, putting her hand on her husband's arm in a show of solidarity. "You've turned out to be the most wicked child, and we will not have you besmirching our good name with your lies or actions."

"Oh yeah? And what will people think when they hear you turned your only daughter out onto the street?" Cassandra counters, unable to keep the note of desperation from her voice.

"What choice do we have when we can't trust her?" her mom responds.

This is really happening. They're really kicking her out. Panic floods her veins. "What's to stop me from reporting your abuse to the cops once you do this?"

Her dad doesn't bat an eye. Instead, he shrugs. "Who would believe the word of a petulant teenager who's just trying to get back at the parents who kicked her out by spreading vicious lies about them?"

Cassandra's shaking her head, unable to believe how he's turning this whole thing around on her. He's right, him acting first does discredit her. Would no one believe her? She's got the scars to prove it.

But does that even matter? She didn't even want to be here twenty minutes ago. Does knowing they don't want her here either change that?

"You know what?" Cassandra says, bitterness raising the

volume of her voice. "Fine. I don't want to be here anyway. And you know what else?" She points her index finger at them like it's a sword. "You claim to have given me everything I could ever want or need. But you never gave me the one thing I've always wanted and needed most. Neither of you are capable of love, and you deserve each other."

With that, she spins on the ball of her foot and storms out of the house. She doesn't care about the clothes or devices or possessions she's leaving behind. She doesn't want any of the crap they bought for her to make up for the love they never gave.

Except for the car. She's not giving up her car. She needs it to get away.

She gets behind the wheel and squeals out of the driveway, racing out of the neighborhood. But where is she going to go? There's HQ, but does she really want to bunk with a couple of teenage boys? Not to mention Logan wouldn't be too keen about that. And it's too early in their relationship for her to ask to stay with him. Suki wouldn't understand the situation, and Cassandra really doesn't want to explain it to her.

There's only one clear choice.

Making up her mind, she turns in the direction of Brielle's house, and she tells herself that she's happy this happened. That the family she thought she had was a lie and that things can only get better.

That the only parents she's ever known casting her aside doesn't hurt like hell.

5

JARETH

"Right now, I'm everything my mother never wanted me to be," Jareth mutters as he draws on the unlit cigarette in his mouth. The end flares thanks to his powers and he creates a small coil of smoke just for extra effect.

Logan glances around surreptitiously. "A middle-aged man in a suit, standing outside a bunch of offices, sucking on a cancer stick?"

"Basically," Jareth huffs. He glances around. "I can't believe you talked me into this. Wait till I see Vee this afternoon."

Logan chuckles a little too loud as he slaps Jareth on the arm. "Because you know this idea is a good one. All the talk happens on the cigarette breaks."

"Just because you're right, doesn't mean I have to like it." Jareth sucks on his cigarette again. Even unlit, he draws in the scent of tobacco and chemicals.

Logan claps his arm again. "You look great for your age, Merv," he says. "Betty-Mae's obviously keeping you on your toes."

"Thanks, I just need to get her off my back about these,"

Jareth says, waving his cigarette around. "Can't a guy have one vice?"

Four agents enter the small courtyard, lighting up their own cigarettes as they stand a few feet away. "You checking out the game this Sunday?"

Logan's eyes flicker toward the men. "Yep, wouldn't miss it."

Three other groups are dotted around, but all they've talked about are barbecues and whether Dave is having an affair with Keith. There's been no mention of the Zodiacs or Solomon or the box.

Jareth draws on his cigarette again, making sure he creates the illusion of the glowing red tip. "I'm thinking of doing ribs in a smoky barbecue sauce."

"Nice," Logan says with a grin. He leans forward a little. "One of those guys is Flanagan. I don't trust him."

Jareth nods, remembering the overweight douche from the lift. He stubs his cigarette out on the ground—another thing that would make his mother shudder—as he casually shifts a little to the right. "Although, maybe I should do a brisket."

"Two are Nebula, two are FBI," Logan says quietly, then quickly chuckles. "As long as you don't turn it into jerky like you did last time."

One of the men coughs, only to draw on his cigarette again. "I thought I was having a quiet afternoon," he mutters, sounding disgruntled.

"Welcome to the real world, Flanagan. Afternoons aren't about naps in your office."

A couple of the others snigger and Jareth almost sighs. If he's created the illusion he's in his mid-forties for nothing...

"Yeah, I'm gonna try and find out what Cadbury's up to. He's spending less and less time at his desk."

Jareth's gaze flies to Logan's. "Bingo," Logan mouths.

"Well, good luck with that. We've got a tip to follow up with a couple of informants."

Flanagan grunts. "Get me a packet of those cheesy buns while you're out."

From the corner of his eye, Jareth sees Flanagan turn away and head back to the FBI building, his coworker by his side. Logan nudges him, indicating they're going to follow.

They've taken two steps when one of the remaining men speaks.

"Do you think this CI has any information on Solomon?"

Jareth stops himself from stilling at the mention of Solomon's name. Logan drops to his knees as he pretends to tie his shoelace. Jareth has to admit he's good.

"We're about to find out," the other responds. "I was kinda hoping for a quiet afternoon."

The first man scoffs. "You're worse than Flanagan." He stubs his cigarette out. "Although I wouldn't mind watching Jack give him the run around again."

The two men chuckle as they, too, head back to the building.

The moment they're alone, Logan turns to Jareth. "We need to split up. I'll follow the Nebula guys, you stay here and see if you can learn anything else."

Jareth's stomach jerks at the suggestion even as he nods. The thought of hanging around the FBI offices on his own isn't a palatable one, but Logan's right, they need to find out as much as they can.

As they follow the others into the building, Logan surreptitiously slips his pass into Jareth's hand. "Just keep it photo side down."

With a quick glance at Jareth, Logan turns right, following the two Nebula operatives out the front doors. Jareth slows his gait as he tries to get his bearings. He's an FBI agent in an FBI building, he needs to act like it.

Up ahead, Flanagan has reached the elevators, so Jareth saunters over, jamming his hands in his pockets as he comes to stand a few feet away. Flanagan glances over his shoulder and Jareth nods at him, glad his sweaty palms are out of sight. Flanagan barely acknowledges him as he turns back.

The elevator doors slide open, and Jareth follows the two men in, his heart thumping in his chest. He focuses on maintaining his illusion as they ascend to the fifth floor. It always gets harder when he's stressed.

All of a sudden, he's not sure this is the best idea. He's not familiar with the layout of this building. He has someone else's pass. And he has no idea what he's doing.

The elevator doors open with a soft *ding* and Flanagan and his friend exit, Jareth behind them. Flanagan juts his chin at his coworker. "Get us a coffee, will you?"

The other man nods, walking straight ahead as Flanagan turns right. Jareth hovers for a moment, unsure where he's supposed to go. It's not like he has an office here.

Flanagan enters a room to his left, leaving the door open. Jareth sees a photocopier not far away and quickly walks over, relieved. He now has a cover.

He grabs a spare sheet of paper and puts it on the glass, frowning as he pretends to press several buttons. Behind him, he hears Flanagan move around his office, lifting the phone from the cradle. He's probably going to call Jack in. Maybe Jareth will find out something interesting and this whole anxiety provoking situation will be worth it.

But the phone is replaced without Flanagan making a call. There are footsteps and Jareth realizes too late what direction Flanagan is heading in. He's exiting his office.

"Need a hand?" Flanagan asks from directly behind him.

Jareth concentrates on maintaining his middle-aged man illusion as he turns around. "Technology, huh?" He smiles as he shakes his head. "Thanks, but I think I've got it figured out."

Except Flanagan doesn't leave. "What's your name? I haven't seen you around."

"Agent Smith," Jareth quickly blurts, inwardly cringing. He just chose the most mundane name ever.

Flanagan steps a little closer. "You new?"

"Ah yeah, just transferred from LA." He grins. "I've heard so much about your bagels. Wanted to try them out myself."

The second man appears, and Jareth notes he's not carrying any coffees. He swallows, realizing something is up.

Flanagan looks like a statue, his face turning hard despite the soft folds. "Is there a reason you're following me, Smith?"

The second man grabs a piece of paper from the copier. "And that you're photocopying blank sheets of paper?"

Jareth's just trying to think of something to create so he can get the pitch out of here when Flanagan shoves a hand into his chest. He pushes him hard and Jareth stumbles back into the office. Another shove and the back of his thighs hit the desk.

He raises his hands to show he's not a threat. "Look guys, it's my first day. I—"

His phone vibrates in his pocket, the sound clattering against the desk. The second agent snatches it out before Jareth can stop him. He reads the screen, then turns it to show Flanagan, his eyes alight with something that has dread snaking down Jareth's spine.

Logan's name is at the top. Underneath is a short message.

I think I have a lead on Solomon.

Flanagan's hand pushes even harder into Jareth's chest as he turns to the other agent. "Bring Logan in."

Then he pushes his face close and Jareth has to contain

his gasp. A silver line circles the operative's irises. He's a Skin.

"We've got a few questions for you," Flanagan growls.

6

TRISTAN

"So, how are we going to find this Klaus guy?" Veronica asks as they climb into Tristan's truck.

He holds up his cell phone. "Actually, I've already emailed him."

"You have?"

Tristan slides his finger over the screen. "That's how Zarius contacted him." He opens his email app. "And I've already spoken to him."

"Surely he didn't just agree to meet with you?" Veronica asks doubtfully.

"Heck no," Tristan says with a chuckle. He shows her the email conversation he had with Klaus yesterday. "I told him I was Zarius's son and that I needed his help decoding a message. He told me he doesn't know a guy called Zarius."

Veronica takes his phone and reads through the messages. "He told you he'll disable this email address if you message him again."

"Yep. Which is why I didn't email again."

"And yet, you're still smiling," Veronica observes. She

narrows her eyes in suspicion. "You know exactly where we're going, don't you?"

Tristan grins. "I've been a clever boy." He takes his phone back, showing an address already typed into the map app. "I bonded with Google and learned how to track the original location of an email via its IP address."

Veronica's brows shoot up. "Impressive."

Tristan wriggles his eyebrows. "I thought so, too." He frowns a little. "Although, I also googled how to crack a code and that didn't get me very far."

"One step at a time, my friend." Veronica clicks her seat-belt in. "So, where are we going?"

"To an internet café close to the city."

She wrinkles her nose. "Mm, seedy."

Tristan starts the truck and pulls out of the driveway. "Which is why I didn't tell anyone until someone had volunteered to come."

Veronica flops into her seat. "I am such a chump."

Chuckling, Tristan follows the instructions of the disembodied female voice of his navigation app. When he sees it's going to be a forty minute drive he suddenly wonders if he's the chump. That's forty minutes that Veronica can grill him about Brielle.

Forty minutes of him evading questions because he doesn't have any answers.

Veronica glances at him, making him tense. "Tell me about Zarius," she says quietly. "I've found since I lost my mom, talking about her keeps the memories alive."

Tristan chews his lip. "He was brave. Determined. And he loved Tess with everything he had."

"Sounds a bit like my dad," Veronica says softly.

Tristan frowns. "I doubt they have much in common." Zarius and Jack Cadbury aren't two people he'd put in the same category, ever.

But Veronica shakes her head. "My dad is just as passionate about his cause as Zarius was." She wrinkles her nose. "He just doesn't realize he's wrong."

Tristan chews on his lip as he considers this. Maybe Veronica has a point. "How did he cope after losing your mom?"

Veronica turns to look out the window. "He didn't. He dedicated himself to protecting the world, as if stopping anyone else's chance of pain could ease his own."

"I don't think I would've liked to have seen Zarius try to live here on Earth without Tess," Tristan says, subdued.

"We had some good times, though," says Veronica, turning back to smile at him. "Mom tried to teach Dad how to make handmade cards once."

Tristan chuckles. "Did it turn out as well as the time Tess tried to teach Zarius how to make scrambled eggs?"

The forty minutes pass quickly, Tristan sharing stories of Zarius and Tess, Veronica reminiscing about her mother and Jack. By the time Tristan parks the truck, he can see what drew Jareth to Veronica. She's confident and bubbly, but also sweet and caring.

They stop outside the door to the internet café. "How do we know Klaus is in there?" Veronica asks.

Tristan shrugs. "We don't. I figure I'll just have to keep coming back here until we find him."

"Great plan," Veronica says with a raised eyebrow.

They step through the door to find a set of stairs heading down. They descend, the lighting becoming poorer the further they go and the smell of stale sweat getting stronger.

"Nice place," Veronica mutters, trying to make sure her shoulder doesn't brush the walls.

The room opens out to reveal several rows of computers, a rumpled couch in the corner with some guy asleep on it with his mouth open, and stained carpet. Tristan and

Veronica sit in mismatched chairs in front of the nearest computers, surreptitiously checking out who's here.

There are three males, all in various stages of disheveled-geek. An old guy is sitting in the back corner, gray hair in a thin ponytail as he hunches over and peers at his screen as if he's forgotten his glasses. There's one female, sitting in the next row, her hair as messy as her clothes.

"Klaus could be female," Veronica whispers.

Tristan nods. Klaus could be any of these people...or none of them.

He logs into the computer he's sitting at, paying for three hours. If they don't find Klaus by then, they'll come back again tomorrow.

With a few quick clicks, Tristan's entered his email server. "Now, to email him one last time."

"Genius," Veronica breathes. "If anyone here gets irate, we know it's Klaus."

"Yep," Tristan chirps cheerily. "Told you I was clever." He quickly types a single line email.

I think we should meet.

He clicks "send" and they scan the room, their breaths held. Nothing happens for long seconds, stretching Tristan's nerves taut. If Klaus isn't here, and he follows through on his threat to disable his email account, then Tristan is going to have to come up with a plan B. A backup plan he hasn't considered yet.

One of the young men two rows over snorts under his breath, moving his mouse with renewed speed. "I'm not a dating service," he mutters.

Bingo!

Tristan and Veronica shoot to their feet, rushing over to sit on either side of him. The guy startles, shoving his glasses up as they slip down his nose. "I don't want any trouble," he squeaks.

Tristan smiles, excited that this fell into place so easily. "Hello, Klaus."

The guy removes his headset, his dark curls springing back into place like those dolls you can't knock over, no matter how hard you try. "I'm sorry, but my name's Jimmy."

"I'm sure you have a lot of names," says Tristan. "But my father knew you as Klaus."

"Look, I don't know who you—"

Tristan leans forward, the urgency of what he needs to do pulsing through him. "Zarius trusted you, and my father trusted few people on this planet. The Zodiacs need your help."

Klaus-Jimmy blinks. "Ah...do you want money? I don't have much, but you can take what you need."

Tristan slams his hand on the table, making the guy jump so hard his glasses slip down again. "I don't have time to play hard to get."

"Tristan," Veronica says quietly. "Maybe he's telling the truth."

Dammit, he should've brought Brielle. If he wasn't so intent on avoiding her, they'd know whether this guy is lying or not. If they let this guy go and he is Klaus, Tristan knows they'll never see him again.

Jaw clenched, Tristan rises to his feet. They're running out of time, he can feel it.

In the back of the room, the old man stands up. "Thanks, Jimmy. You did good." He looks at Tristan. "I'm Klaus."

Tristan's too stunned to move for a moment, but he quickly regains his wits. He strides over to the old man. "You set us up?"

Klaus raises a gray eyebrow. "Of course I set you up. I had to make sure you were who you said you were."

"Impressive," Veronica says, joining them. "You knew

Tristan would track your IP address here. That he'd try the email, seeing if he could catch the receiver."

"If I didn't want you to find my IP address, you wouldn't have," Klaus says with all the superiority of someone who knows what IP address stands for. He turns back to Tristan. "And it was unusual that Zarius didn't contact me himself."

Tristan feels his soul sag. "That's because he and Tess are dead. Killed."

"I'm sorry to hear that," Klaus says somberly. "Zarius was a good man."

Tristan nods, acknowledging the understatement. "So, you'll help us?"

"What do you need?"

Tristan holds up a thumb drive. "We've intercepted a code. We need to know what it says."

The fate of the Universe might depend on it.

Klaus takes it and inserts it into the computer he was sitting at. The screen goes black, filling with several lines of jargon, exactly what Tristan's been staring at for days. A moment later Klaus starts typing, his fingers flying over the keyboard with impressive speed.

He squints as he leans closer, his fingers never losing momentum. "It seems to contain several Caesar shifts within the same message," he mutters.

Tristan glances at Veronica and they both shrug. Klaus's screen steadily fills up with more numbers and letters and weird-looking symbols.

Klaus frowns. "Nope, not a Caesar cipher. Is it some sort of RSA encryption?" He types some more. "Surely it's not digraph…"

Tristan pulls up a chair, indicating for Veronica to do the same. He's willing to sit here as long as it takes.

Except only half an hour has passed when Klaus leans back, rubbing his eyes. "This could take years."

"What?" asks Tristan, alarmed. "We don't have weeks, let alone years."

He needs this message decoded yesterday.

Klaus shakes his head. "This is a complex code. There's grid transposition, some sort of substitution, heck, I think they've thrown in some binary just for fun."

"And?" Veronica asks. "What does that mean?"

"It's a combination cipher of some sort. You're going to need a key."

Tristan frowns. "A key?"

"Yep. This is one hell of an algorithm. The key is what will crack your code for you. It's like the instruction book, the '3 is C' kind of thing."

"Where do I find that?"

"You're going to need a hacker. A good one." Tristan's about to point out he thought that's what Klaus was for, but the older man lifts his hand. "Someone better than me."

"Surely no one could be better than you," Veronica says warmly.

Klaus sniffs as he flicks his thin gray ponytail. "Very few." He blinks, as if he just realized even someone his age isn't immune to flattery from a pretty girl. "But if you want it done quick, you're going to have to find them."

Frustration winds through Tristan's muscles. How long is that going to take? "Do you know anyone?"

"Only by name," Klaus says. His voice dips as he tucks his head down. "Dyad."

Tristan jolts in surprise. "The same Dyad from UFOfanatics.com?"

"You know him?" Klaus asks, looking as taken aback as Veronica.

"Well, yeah. I monitor all the major alien websites. The forum is quite active on this one, and it's moderated by someone called Dyad."

"Dyad is one of the best hackers I know," says Klaus. "But he's deeper than the deep web. You're not going to find him easily."

Tristan sighs. When was anything easy when it came to getting answers about this code?

Suddenly, Klaus's computer screen turns off. Klaus slaps his hands on his knees as he pushes himself upright. "Well, that's it for me."

"You're leaving?" Tristan asks incredulously.

"Sorry, I never spend longer than an hour at any one computer," Klaus responds, not looking in the least apologetic. "Places to go, authorities to avoid, you know how it is."

"But—"

"I've done all I can." Klaus's wrinkled face brightens as he smiles. "Think of me as a link, the stepping stone that leads you to your next step."

Finding Dyad.

Tristan nods, acknowledging the man is probably right. He stands and extends his hand. "Thank you. You've been very helpful."

Klaus doesn't hesitate in shaking it. "Any son of Zarius's is a friend of mine." With a quick salute at Veronica, he makes his way to the steps, bounding up them in a way that makes Tristan wonder exactly how old Klaus is.

Veronica turns to Tristan. "So, Dyad huh?"

Tristan sits back down and logs onto the computer he's at. "Yeah. The creator of UFOfanatics." He quickly navigates to the website. "I haven't checked in for a while, like so many of these websites, it was starting to fill up with badly photoshopped images and conspiracy theories."

Veronica leans over his shoulder as he clicks on the login page. "You're a member?"

"I've joined most of these websites." Always looking for anything that hinted at pods or Zodiac powers. "If you want to read personal accounts of abductions and probing, these are the places to be," he adds wryly.

Veronica wrinkles her nose. "I'll keep that in mind." Her eyebrows hike up as she sees him enter his username. "GeminiI?"

Tristan doesn't answer. He's not going to explain that a small part of him was hoping a GeminiII would one day send him a message.

"We need to get Dyad curious." He considers his choice of words for a few moments then quickly types.

Dyad. You up for a challenge? Got an unbreakable code. Alien origins.

Tristan posts it to the forum. He lets out a breath, glancing at Veronica. "Now we do the part I hate."

Veronica lets out her own huff as she flops into her chair. "Wait."

7

ADA

"The FBI's received a code," Ada murmurs, her gaze focused on Esther's screen as she sits cross-legged on the hood of their car. She turns her shocked gaze to Eric. "It came through a wormhole."

Eric tucks his hands into his pockets as he leans against the car beside her, looking thoughtful. "It's a message."

Ada clutches the locket at her throat, excitement thrumming through her veins. "We need to find out what it says."

"I had a feeling you'd say that," he sighs.

"We have to, Eric! This is what we've been looking for!"

Eric scuffs his shoe over one of the tufts of grass peeking through the cracks in the asphalt of the empty parking lot they're in. "It's also the FBI, Ada." He glances up, concern shifting through his wintergreen eyes. "Dyad is on their most wanted list."

Ada puts Esther aside and slides down the hood to stand in front of him. "And they've never got so much as a gossamer thread, let alone a lead on me."

His hands come to rest on her hips as he sighs. "I don't know what you're planning, but I don't like it."

Slipping in closer, Ada winds her arms around his shoulders, still noticing how well they fit, even after all their time together. "Don't you want answers, Eric?" she asks quietly. "Don't you want to know?"

They left the group home as soon as they could for a reason. They're both different. And they've never been able to find out why.

He rests his forehead against hers, his familiar scent filling her lungs. "You know I do." He sighs, drawing her in even closer. "Maybe then we could actually…"

He doesn't finish the sentence, but he doesn't need to. Maybe they could get further than first base without Ada triggering her powers and Eric having to use his to deal with the collateral damage.

Ada winds her fingers through the hair at the nape of his neck. "That's why I applied for a job."

Eric's head lifts so he can study her better. "A job…" he repeats, clearly suspicious. "Where?"

"As a mail boy, totally sexist language by the way, but I figured if everyone seems to assume Dyad is a guy, then maybe I'm destined for male vocations."

Eric waits, knowing her well enough to tell that she's hedging. His fingers tighten around her waist as if he's bracing himself.

Ada sighs. "I applied for a job at the FBI office."

"You what?" Eric explodes in disbelief.

"It makes sense," she rushes in. "It'll be so much easier to hack their system from within their walls. I get my hands on the code and I'll be out of there, I promise."

"You're going into the enemy's headquarters!"

Ada grins. "I know. Hiding in plain sight and all that. It's totally something Dyad would do."

Eric opens his mouth to object again but she places a finger over his lips, feeling his frustrated huff.

"We need answers, Eric. And this is the only way we can get them."

Ada holds her breath, and a second later his body unwinds, resignation pulling the edges of his lips down. "You get the code and you get the hell out of there."

She nods solemnly. "I promise. Believe me, I don't want to spend any more time there than I have to."

Eric's face twists with pain. "If anything happened to you, Ada…"

She curls into him, knowing the agony it would be if the tables were turned and she lost him. They've been each other's everything for so long now. They're soulmates.

"I won't ever leave you," she promises, her voice full of the love she feels for this sweet, loyal, strong guy who has her heart.

He presses a kiss to her head. "I'm counting on that."

Esther dings from where she's still sitting on the hood of the car, telling Ada she has a notification. Ada pulls back. "Maybe that's an email telling me I've got the job."

Eric rolls his eyes. "As much as I've tried to encourage you to find more regular, legal employment, this is one job I hope you don't get."

Ada quickly enters her password—a fifteen character mix of meaningless words with numbers substituted for several letters—and looks to see what's come in. Disappointment stabs when she sees it's not an email from the FBI.

She huffs. According to the fake resume she created, she's over-qualified for the job.

Instead, it's an email telling her of a message. She glances at Eric. "It's from UFOfanatics."

He leans back against the car, no longer as interested. "From the three-eyed alien who works at the Pentagon again?"

Ada throws him a quick smile. "She's having great difficulty finding glasses that fit properly." She clicks on the email and frowns. "But no, it's not her."

Eric joins her, looking over her shoulder. "What is it?"

They both read the single line message.

Dyad. You up for a challenge? Got an unbreakable code. Alien origins.

Eric lets out a slow whistle. "They can't be talking about the same code."

Ada shakes her head so hard her curls whip her cheeks. "It's a trap." She slams Esther shut so hard she winces. "Sorry, girl."

Eric comes around to face her. "You're not going to answer?"

"No way. That's exactly what they want me to do."

Eric frowns as he grips her hand. "But if they have the code, you won't need to go into the FBI offices."

"If this is a trap, it's no safer."

"But—"

"No, Eric," Ada says, wanting him to understand. "I do this on my terms, not theirs."

Eric looks at her for long moments before his shoulders drop. "Okay, we do it your way."

Ada launches herself at him, throwing her arms around his neck. Eric catches her, like he always does. Always has.

And always will.

She kisses him, making sure to keep the contact brief. "It's going to be fine, you'll see."

Eric nods even though she can see he's not totally convinced. "So, where to now?"

Ada glances at the afternoon sun, knowing as well as Eric that there's no time to find somewhere new to play house. "Looks like we're sleeping rough for the moment."

Eric's arms loosen as he steps away. As much as Ada wants to keep holding him, as much as she resents the coolness replacing all the places their bodies touched, she lets him. Tonight is going to be tough and they could both use the space.

They'll park somewhere, maybe even here in this abandoned parking lot, and sleep in the car. She dreads it almost as much as she looks forward to it. Being with Eric is as natural as breathing. Even in the group home they would sneak into each other's rooms so they could sleep together.

But they're not kids anymore. They're in love. Cuddles and chaste kisses stopped being enough long ago.

And tucked into the backseat, is all that cramped space. So much of her touching him.

And nothing they can do about it.

Ada's hands ball into fists, her hands hardening in the same way her determination does. The sooner they have answers about who they are and why she's like this, the better.

BRIELLE

The sound of arguing muffled by a layer of wood and glass greets Brielle before she reaches the front door of her house. She's never heard Frank or Bea's voices raised like this, and the anxiety she already had after Frank's text quadruples.

What could have them so worked up? Did they find out about who and what she is? Find something of Tristan's in the attic?

With a trembling hand, she turns the knob and opens the door.

Frank's fingers are raking his scalp, and Bea presses one hand to her forehead with the other propped on her hip, their loud exchange stopping when they see her.

"What's going on?" Brielle asks slowly, terrified of what the answer will be.

"The IRS seized all my firm's assets," Frank says, his voice animated yet dry. "They accused me of embezzling funds from my clients. I could go to jail."

"Omigod!" Brielle exclaims. The questions jump out of her mouth as soon as they pop into her mind. "How did this happen? Why do they think that? What are we going to do?"

Frank steps backward and falls into a chair at the kitchen table, looking older than she's ever seen him. He shakes his head. "I don't know."

Brielle remembers her lie detection alarm when the Sinclairs came over for dinner. How he promised something about the clients. And she's certain this is his doing.

"It's Mr. Sinclair," she thinks out loud. "He did this. He made the merger with your firm so that he could embezzle the funds and frame you for it."

Frank shakes his head, doubt wrinkling his already furrowed brow. But after a few seconds, the wrinkles smooth as understanding dawns. He looks at Bea. "You don't think..."

She shrugs, her dismay making her usually straight brown hair wiry and frizzy.

"I knew it," Brielle mutters, angry at herself for not trying harder to intervene. "I knew he was up to something, and I didn't try hard enough to stop it."

A forceful knock at the front door makes all their heads turn. The clouds outside darken, casting a foreboding gray haze on the kitchen walls.

Bea hesitantly answers the door, and when she opens it, two police officers don't wait for an invitation to barge into the kitchen, one of them pulling out handcuffs.

"Frank Pierce, you're under arrest for embezzlement and fraud," he announces as they go behind Frank and slap the cuffs on his wrists.

"God, this can't be happening," he says in a hoarse whisper, then grunts as the cop gruffly pulls him by the cuffs toward the door.

"Frank, what do I do?" Bea pleads as they cart him out of the house and toward the cop car in the driveway.

"Find evidence that I'm innocent," he says. "And get me a good lawyer!" he calls as they tuck his head into the backseat.

Brielle and Bea watch from the porch as the cop car whisks Frank away to an uncertain fate and disappears into the distance. They remain there, crickets serenading them with a steady soothing song that deceivingly portrays the world as being safe, normal, peaceful.

But everything is far from safe, normal or peaceful.

"I can't believe this is happening," Bea says in little more than a whisper.

"What do we do?" Brielle asks again.

Bea cradles the top of her forehead with both hands and begins to pace back and forth. "I'll make some calls. I must have some friends who can refer me to some lawyers." She stops and looks at Brielle, her eyes so wide that Brielle can see the red veins that stress has made visible in the whites of her eyes. "You've been doing paperwork with Frank. Can you search for any evidence that he didn't do anything illegal?"

Brielle nods, thrilled to have a job to do.

They turn to rush inside, Bea dialing the phone with the speed of a ninja, and Brielle desperately searching through files in Frank's office for anything they might have missed.

As she scans page after page, a seething in her chest intensifies. Cassandra's dad did this. She's certain of it. There's no way Frank would ever steal from anyone. He's too kind. And it's too coincidental that this accusation would happen only after the merger was completed between the two companies.

Cassandra's dad planned this right from the start. He just needed a fall guy. But how is she going to prove it?

Brielle wasn't the type to judge easily, or to hold grudges. She typically believed that everyone was essentially good inside, that people made mistakes and deserved second chances. But she'd seen into Richard Sinclair's soul, or the lack thereof, and she's certain that there is absolutely nothing redeemable inside him. He is a wicked, selfish and toxic human being, who had not only terrorized her oldest friend for over a decade, but had now thrown a wrench into the only family she's ever had.

She doesn't like to even think of the word "hate", but she can't keep her teeth from grinding.

Knock, knock.

Brielle looks up from the paper mess on Frank's desk to see Cassandra in the doorway.

"Can I stay with you for a few days? Mom and Dad kicked me out." Cassandra's face is a mask, but Brielle can see through the façade. Cassandra is breaking up inside.

Brielle rushes to hug her. "Of course, you can. Stay with us for as long as you need."

Cassandra returns the hug, and the shakiness of the breath she lets out tells Brielle the volume of her relief, and the frailty of her confidence.

Screw it, she's going to think it.

I hate Richard Sinclair.

CASSANDRA

C assandra fights back the urge to cry as she withdraws from Brielle's embrace. "Thanks."

"What happened?" Brielle asks, brows knitted with worry.

"Well, a few days ago, I confessed everything to my mom," Cassandra explains. She shakes her head. "She didn't believe me. Not even when I—" She stops herself, unwilling to share the part about the scars on her back. It doesn't matter that Brielle has seen a few on her arm, or that Brielle knows the depth of her dad's abuse. Some fragile, desperate part of her won't allow the exposure of those scars to anyone else.

Brielle doesn't question Cassandra's pause. She just waits patiently for Cassandra to continue.

"Then my dad found out we'd been inside his office and accused me of stealing something," she goes on. "Which, technically, we didn't do," she adds, holding up her index finger. "My mom totally took his side, saying how they can't trust me and that I'm making up lies. They told me I was no longer welcome under their roof."

The crease in Brielle's brow deepens. "Oh, Cassie, I'm so sorry." She puts a comforting hand on Cassandra's shoulder.

"What does this mean for your adoption? Are they going to annul it? Will you have to go back to the orphanage? Or into foster care?"

"I don't know." Cassandra hadn't wanted to think that far. "Tristan and Jareth live on their own. I'm sure I can find a way to legally emancipate myself. But I'm close enough to eighteen that hopefully it won't come to that."

Suddenly, she realizes that she may not even know her true age. That none of them do. Who knows exactly how old any of them were when they were sent to Earth, except for Tristan, who, from his stories, had only just been born right before. The age she thinks she is might be totally wrong, and there's no way the birthdate on her birth certificate could be accurate.

Cassandra shrugs and scoffs. "Whatever. It's probably better this way. That house hasn't felt like home in ages anyway. My dad's been avoiding me and my mom pretended I was invisible. I hated being there, so now I don't have to. I'm set free!" She throws up her hands.

The pout in Brielle's lower lip is more pronounced, as if she doesn't believe Cassandra's proclamation of relief. But then she remembers that Brielle can sense lies. If Brielle doesn't believe it, then maybe, deep down, Cassandra doesn't either...

"Well, it's really not the best time, but I'm sure Bea will let you stay here as long as you need," Brielle offers, and for the first time Cassandra registers the state of the house, the more than usual angst in Brielle's body language, and the frazzled way Brielle's mom had been talking on the phone when she waved Cassandra into the house.

"What's going on?" she asks.

A staunch expression flattens Brielle's features and pales her complexion. She visibly swallows and looks away. "Frank was just arrested."

"What?" Cassandra exclaims. "For what?"

"The IRS claims that Frank embezzled from his clients."

"Do you think he did?" Cassandra presses. She feels bad for bursting in with her sob story without even asking Brielle what was happening. She's a terrible friend. Maybe her mom was right about her selfishness.

Brielle slowly shakes her head. "There's no way Frank would ever do something like that. But I know somebody who would." She sheepishly raises her eyes to meet Cassandra's.

Understanding sparks like a match in a dark cave, and Cassandra gasps. "Holy crap! My dad framed yours!"

"My thoughts exactly," Brielle says, nodding and pursing her lips.

Cassandra grips both of Brielle's upper arms. "We have to expose him."

"How are we going to do that? He just kicked you out, and I'm the daughter of the man he framed. I highly doubt he's going to let either of us even remotely close to him."

Cassandra shakes her head, chewing on her cheek as she ponders. "This can't all be just coincidence. The timing is too convenient. First the thing with Solomon and the box, now the charges. It has to all be linked somehow."

Brielle frowns. "You think the frame job has something to do with Solomon?"

Cassandra shrugs. "I don't know, but I feel like there has to be some connection. My dad went out of his way to hire a shady lawyer to get you out of FBI interrogation, and then that same lawyer holds Logan's dad hostage for a mystery box inside an alien space pod none of us knew about. Then the next thing we know, your dad gets framed for fraud. You know what all these things have in common?"

Brielle looks at her expectantly, waiting for her to spell it out.

"You," Cassandra answers, waving her hand at Brielle. "My dad is clearly linked to Chardis, and for some reason, he has a weird interest in you. I'm willing to bet that he'll talk to you if you approach him."

Brielle begins to shake her head. "We've already established that I don't have the ability to fake anything."

"Then don't fake it," Cassandra says. "Be as honest as you can without giving anything away. He wants something from you, and we have to let him think he's going to get it. We'll go to his office tomorrow, and while you're fishing for information, I'll snoop around and see if I can find proof that he framed your dad."

Shadows of doubt play on Brielle's face as she deliberates this. "You really think that will work?"

"It's our best shot," Cassandra replies. "Besides, if we get caught, what's the worst he can do? He's already disowned me. There's nothing else that man can do to hurt me."

And darned if she's not going to do everything in her to make sure he pays for all of it.

JACK

15:52

"Dammit," Jack growls, his hands on his hips as he turns slowly in the vacant living room he's standing in.

He knew the chances of Solomon being at his residential address were slim, but he'd hoped there would be some evidence to find. But the place is like a sterile hospital wing. Worse.

There are no prints.

No hair fragments.

No leads.

He grabs his antacids and pops two in his mouth. He's about to put the bottle back in his pocket when he decides to have a third. He's going to need it. As he grinds them into a paste in his mouth, he wonders what the hell he's supposed to do next.

As if answering his question, his cell phone rings, Logan's name flashing on the front.

"Hey," he barks, then quickly modulates his tone. His son is one of the few people on his side. "What's up?"

"I'm just at the park off the main street. Was wondering if you wanted to catch up for a hot dog or something."

Jack's heartburn eases a little and he knows it's not just the antacids. "Sure, son. I'm just in the city, so it might take forty-five minutes to get there."

"I can wait," Logan says lightly. "It would be good to catch up away from the office."

Where anyone could be listening. "Smart thinking," Jack agrees. "I'm leaving now."

They hang up and Jack lets out a slow breath. With the changes in the wormhole and the message that they're still trying to decipher, he knows something is up. That something is coming. But he's decided to honor the truce with Tristan and the others, for now.

As much as he wishes otherwise, Tristan saved his life.

And although Veronica gave him that thumb drive full of information on some pretty big name criminals, Jack hasn't forgotten that she's dating Jareth.

Logan, on the other hand, has continued to date that Cassandra girl, just so they can keep secret tabs on Tristan. The truce doesn't mean he needs to totally back off.

Which leaves Logan as the one person he trusts.

Jack strides for the door, his footsteps echoing through

the vacant apartment. Nebula needs to find Solomon before anyone else does, and Logan can help him do that.

Solomon has the box.

And Jack will bet every last antacid on this planet that what's inside it is more dangerous than anything humans have ever seen before.

LOGAN

L ogan hangs up, staring at his cell phone for long moments. The guilt that's slithering through his gut isn't pleasant. Almost painful.

Even knowing this is what he has to do, that millions of sentient lives depend on it, doesn't help.

He jams the phone back into his pocket, slipping further behind the tree he's leaning against. Shrubbery engulfs him as the two Nebula operatives he followed here come down the path, telling Logan that his guess paid off. This is a secluded corner of the park where his father has met his CIs before. Apart from the odd dog walker, most people prefer to stay closer to the lake and play equipment.

One of the operatives lights a cigarette while the other slips his hands into his pocket, looking like two men casually taking a break. But Logan can sense their edginess, notices the way their gazes keep flickering around him. They're tense and waiting for something.

That something ambles down the path a few minutes later. Two men, one tall and overweight, the other short and stocky, approach the agents.

The first operative offers them a cigarette and the men both take one. There's silence as two more glowing tips are added to the first.

The moment smoke coils into the air, the second operative speaks. "So, you got something on Solomon?"

"He's a slippery eel, but we think we got a lead," says the tall one.

Even from this distance Logan can sense the flash of frustration. The man could be lying. CIs know they don't get paid unless they have information.

"Yeah? What sort of lead?"

Before Logan can hear a response, a hand clamps over his mouth and he's jerked roughly backward. He thrashes, throwing his arms out and kicking wildly. But whoever has him is stronger than he expected. His arms are yanked back painfully, the hand over his mouth only tightening as he tries to call out.

A second man appears and grabs his legs. Twisting as he desperately tries to free himself, Logan's carried further into the woodland surrounding the park. At first he thinks this is some sort of mugging, but he quickly notices the two men are wearing suits. As he kicks out with his legs at the man holding them, he sees the jacket part, revealing a flash of badge.

These guys are FBI.

The woods thicken and the shadows deepen as the agents carry him as if he weighs little more than a sack of potatoes. Logan tries to call out, but he's muffled by the hand over his mouth. The further he's taken, the more he realizes he's no longer going to be heard.

"This'll do," growls the second man.

He releases Logan's legs and the first man slams him against a tree trunk, knocking his breath from his lungs. The other agent quickly slips behind him and before Logan can realize what's happening, his hands are cuffed behind his back.

The first man releases his suffocating palm from over Logan's mouth. "You scream and—"

Logan draws in a quick breath and tries to shout as loud as he can. The sound is instantly severed when a fist ploughs into his stomach. He groans, trying to double over except he's still being pinned against the tree.

"Good point," the man sneers. "Sometimes showing is better than telling."

He pushes his face close to Logan's. "Now, what did the message say?"

Logan focuses through the pain, wishing he could draw away from the hot air gusting over him. Involuntarily, he draws in a sharp breath of his own. There's a thin silver ring around the man's irises. Logan hasn't seen it before, but Tristan has told him about it.

Skins.

The man slams Logan against the tree as if he's planning on shaking the information out of him. "Well? Where's the key?"

"Go to hell," spits Logan.

The agent holding him glances over his shoulder at his comrade. "He's playing hard to get."

The Skin approaches, smiling. "My favorite type of hostage."

Without even a blink to warn Logan, the Skin's fist slams across his jaw, snapping his head against the tree. But the Skin doesn't stop there. He pummels Logan's face, his chest, his stomach. Agony explodes with each strike, but pinned against the trunk, Logan is little more than a punching bag.

Stepping back, the Skin adjusts his cuffs, his breathing as even as when he started. "Sometimes they just need to be softened up a bit."

"Now," the first one says. "Where is the key?"

Through the haze of pain, Logan tries to sense what these men are feeling. Maybe he can dial it down, take some of the sting out of their blows. He just needs a little time to think.

Except what he detects has his stomach heaving with fresh nausea. These men are feeling glee. They're excited at the prospect of violence.

For the first time since he was taken, a frission of fear trickles down Logan's spine. These Skins are willing to kill.

"Well?" the Skin shakes Logan's bruised body. "We need the key!"

Logan spits out a mouthful of blood. "Even if I knew, I wouldn't tell you."

The Skin standing behind the one holding him smiles. No, grins. His delight flashes even brighter.

The first one jerks Logan closer. "I was kinda hoping you'd say that. Let's bring him in."

His fist bulldozes into Logan's face and everything goes black.

11

JARETH

The screams that reach Jareth through the walls of the interrogation room he's sitting in have ice spearing through his veins. They're so laced with pain it makes his marrow quiver.

Jareth jolts as he recognizes the voice. They're Logan's screams.

He shoots to his feet, now even less okay with being in here. Flanagan and his douche offsider threw him in after cornering him, promising they'll be back. Jareth's not sure what their ploy is, but if it's making them wait, it's a good one.

Spending this whole time maintaining his middle-aged agent illusion is progressively draining him. If Flanagan and his friend decide to get physical, he doubts he'd be able to maintain it.

And then Jareth's Zodiac identity will be blown.

But right now, he has more important things to worry about. Logan's been captured and is going through his own interrogation.

Jareth presses himself against the door, catching narrow

glimpses of the corridor he was dragged down through the tiny window. To the right it's empty. To the left, Flanagan and his friend are approaching. They walk and chat as if they can't hear the blood curdling screams that are piercing the air.

Jareth knows he has to act quickly. He ducks down, tucking himself behind where the door will open. Concentrating, he projects an image of middle-aged him sitting in the seat where Flanagan left him.

There's the *beep* of a pass over a detector and the door unlocks. It's pushed open and Jareth flattens himself against the wall.

"So, Smith. You ready to talk?" Flanagan booms. "Cause whatever's happening in room three could easily happen to you."

The moment the men have entered, Jareth darts around the door. He slams it closed behind him. A quick kick to the sensor pad and the surface cracks, the light beneath dying out.

"Hey!" the two agents shout.

But Jareth doesn't wait to see their shocked faces. He needs to get to room three. The screams die away and Jareth quickens his step. He never thought that nerve wracking sound would be preferable to silence, but screams mean Logan's alive.

Silence creates the possibility that he's not.

Room three is only a few doors down. The screams pick up again just as Jareth reaches it. He bangs on the door, cutting the agonizing sounds short.

A burly face appears in the small window. "What?"

For once, Jareth is glad he chose the illusion that coats his face. He scowls, looking every bit the imposing older man he needs to be. "The boss wants a word."

"We're busy."

"Flanagan's orders," Jareth barks.

The man sneers. "This interrogation is also Flanagan's orders."

"Just go see what he wants, will ya?" Jareth demands. A bead of sweat trickles down his temple. His illusion is getting harder and harder to maintain. "I need to get him off my back."

The goon hesitates and Jareth holds his breath. A moment later there's a *beep* and a *click*. The instant the door opens a crack, Jareth shoves.

The goon stumbles. "Hey—"

But that gap is all Jareth needs. Everything Tristan has taught him rushes to the forefront of his mind.

Punches to certain parts of the body are going to give you far more bang for your buck.

The blow to the goon's throat has the man reeling backward, clutching his neck as choking sounds sputter past his lips. The second goon leaps from where he was standing beside Logan, holding his head by his hair. Logan's head drops back down where he's slumped in a chair, his face puffy and bruised.

The second goon leaps at Jareth, growling like a feral animal. Jareth ducks as a massive fist swings at his head, bringing an uppercut into the man's gut. The goon barely grunts.

Which means he's a Skin, just as Jareth suspected.

He raises his fists, pretending he's on the offensive, when really, he's on the defense. After maintaining the illusion for so long, Jareth can feel his energy waning. Even if he could think of an illusion that would distract the Skin, he won't be able to create it. He's going to have to fight. And just like the first guy, he has to make his first blow count.

Look for the signal they're about to move.

Just as Tristan's words slip through Jareth's mind, the Skin's face twists. He surges forward a split-second later, but thanks to the advice, Jareth is ready. He spins and kicks.

Knocking someone right on the jaw hinge, just below the ear, can break their jaw and end most fights in an instant.

His foot connects with the side of the Skin's head, making it whiplash to the side. The Skin grunts then rights himself. When he turns back to Jareth, his jaw is hanging at an odd angle, distorting his face. He shakes his head as he growls deep in his throat, seemingly impervious to his jaw moving of its own accord.

Sometimes one strike won't be enough. These asshats don't feel pain like the rest of us.

Jareth races to find his fading energy. He shouldn't have waited. He should've followed through.

The Skin launches at him again, fury filling his eyes with an unholy light. The pain has only fed his anger. He throws a punch which Jareth instinctively blocks, surprising even himself. The muscle memory that Tristan spoke of must be kicking in.

But then there's another punch, and another, and another. Jareth retreats, blocking the second and the third. The fourth finds its target, slamming into his chest and knocking the wind out of him.

He stumbles backward, fear choking him just as much as the blow. He's not a fighter. Never has been.

Just as the Skin is preparing to strike again, he crumples, revealing Logan standing behind him. His bruised face twists with a grin, blood trickling from a cut on his temple and he's cradling his arm against his chest. "Offensive strategies 101. Hitting someone at the base of the skull can short circuit their spinal cord. It's the most effective place to strike."

Jareth straightens, seeing that the first Skin is out cold,

too. "Replace 'Zarius said' at the beginning of that sentence and you just sounded like Tristan."

Logan tenses, grabbing Jareth's arm. "We need to get out of here. They're waking up." He draws Jareth with him as he maneuvers to the door. "And even barely awake, they're far from happy."

They dart through the door and Logan slams it closed behind them. Jareth quickly kicks the sensor pad again, small sparks shooting out as it short circuits.

"How do we get out of here?" he asks.

Logan frowns, glancing up and down the corridor. "Where are we?"

Alarm shoots down Jareth's spine. "In the FBI building. These must be their interrogation rooms."

Logan swallows. "I've never been here before. I'm Nebula now, not FBI."

A *thud* echoes from the door beside them, making both Jareth and Logan leap away from it. The Skins are trying to get out.

"This way," Jareth says, turning right. Although he has no idea where he's going, this is the direction Flanagan brought him in. It has to lead to the exit.

They break into a run, Logan hobbling from his injuries, Jareth already panting as he struggles to maintain his disguise.

Behind them, the *thumps* grow louder. Jareth glances over his shoulder, his heart a freight train in his chest. There's a thundering *boom* and the door erupts open, the two Skins now free. What's more, Flanagan's blasts open, and they join the first two Skins.

"Run!" he shouts.

They inject as much speed as they can into their bruised and exhausted bodies. They reach the end of the corridor where it splits left and right. Jareth desperately tries to remember which way Flanagan brought him, but he was almost as terrified then as he is now. The hallways were quickly blending into each other.

Knowing they can't afford to slow down, Jareth turns left. They've only run a few yards when he realizes his mistake. The corridor ends, several doors on either side.

"It's a dead end!" Logan pants painfully.

Jareth tries the first door. Locked. The second and third. Both locked. He tries the fourth even though he knows it's a waste of time, but he's desperate.

Also locked.

They spin around as they hear the ominous drumbeat of boots coming down the corridor. Jareth and Logan come to stand side by side, their fists up and their bodies ready to fight. Maybe, between Zarius's advice and Logan's training, they stand a chance.

Flanagan appears, three Skins behind him. He sneers as he realizes what Jareth wishes wasn't true.

They're trapped.

Two of the Skins move to either side of Flanagan, creating a wall of evil.

He smiles, even his jowls lifting. "We haven't finished our questioning. This time, we won't be gentle."

"This time, we're not coming with you." But even as Logan growls the words, he sways. He's weaker than Jareth thought.

Jareth works to steady his out of control pulse. This isn't going to end well, but he's not going down without putting up a darned good fight.

"Take them alive," orders Flanagan as he steps backward.

The Skins' faces light with excitement as they launch at Jareth and Logan. Logan does the same, showing he's not going to sit back and wait for the fight to come to him. He lands a couple of punches before the Skin he's fighting powers a fist into his face. Logan crumples with a pained groan.

Jareth is standing over him in a blink. He's terrified, he doesn't stand a chance against three Skins, but Logan is a Zodiac.

He's family.

The Skin grins. "One down, another to go. This is going to be over far too quickly."

Another joins him. "You need to share the fun."

They both move simultaneously, the same sick expression of anticipation on their faces. Jareth braces himself. If he can do like Logan and get a few blows in before he's taken down, then he'll take it.

A gunshot cracks through the hallway. "Stop," roars a voice Jareth recognizes.

Flanagan and the Skins spin around, seeing what Jareth's already registered. Jack Cadbury is running down the hall, several agents with him. Each of them has a gun drawn.

The Skins slowly put their hands up, and Flanagan does the same a moment later.

"Against the wall! Now!" shouts Jack.

The men do as they're told, hatred sparking from their eyes.

"Secure them," Jack growls as he strides straight past them. Jareth steps back as Jack kneels beside his son. "Logan?"

Logan stirs, blinking up through a black eye. More blood is streaked across his face. "Dad?"

Relief slides through Jack's gaze, but it's short lived. He turns to face the men, his movements slow and controlled.

"You interrogated my son?" he asks, his voice laced with fury.

Flanagan winces as his hands are cuffed behind his back. "Have you asked him what he knows?" he spits. "Have you even considered that maybe he's learned more than he's told you?"

Jack launches to his feet and his fist slams into Flanagan's soft face. Flanagan's head snaps backward, crimson blood flowing down his mouth and chin.

He shakes off the blow as if it was a slap. "I'll take that as a no."

Jack's about to hit him again when Logan calls out. "Dad, he's trying to get to you."

Jack hesitates then steps back. "Lock them up," he says, his body vibrating with anger. "We'll make sure they have what's coming to them."

The agents, no doubt Nebula, muscle Flanagan and his Skins away. Jareth leans against the wall, suddenly dizzy. He can feel his disguise fading. He has minutes, maybe less before Jack sees who he is.

Jack crouches back down beside Logan. "When you didn't show up at the park, I suspected something was up. But not this…"

Logan pushes himself up, drawing up a crooked smile. "Thanks for saving our asses."

Jack glances at Jareth, as if he just realized they're not alone. "Who's this?"

"Agent Smith," says Jareth, still breathing a little heavily. At least it maintains his disguise as a middle-aged man. "I heard your son being questioned. Let's just say they weren't following protocol."

Jack nods, his eyes filling with gratitude. "Thank you." He frowns a little. "I haven't seen you before, Smith."

Logan gets to his feet, using his father as a crutch. "Dad, we need to talk." He glances at Jareth meaningfully. "Alone."

Relief courses through Jareth as he jumps at the reprieve

Logan just gave him. "Agent, you know where to find me." He strides down the corridor, following the sounds of the men's footsteps. "And you know what?" he calls over his shoulder. "First thing I'm doing is filling out the paperwork to transfer back to Seattle."

12

TRISTAN

Tristan taps the edge of the laptop. "I really thought Dyad would've taken the bait by now."

"It's been a day," Veronica points out, spinning idly on her chair as they sit in HQ.

Logan and Jareth are out following feds. Brielle and Cassandra are dealing with family issues that he's yet to get the low down on but is reluctant to ask questions. Tristan's conscious that they have their own lives. One that doesn't include him or the Zodiacs.

And he has to respect that. Especially for the girl he has feelings for but can't do anything about. Which just makes it next level complicated.

And while all this is happening, Tristan's sitting here, waiting for a message.

When time is running out.

"Screw this," he mutters, opening up a new tab. "I'm going to email Klaus."

Veronica stops her spinning. "But he said he'd disable the email account after your last one. I don't think he wants to be found."

"Well, if it bounces, then I've got my answer," Tristan says grimly. He's getting desperate.

No response from Dyad. I need to find him.

Tristan clicks send, realizing he's holding his breath. If he gets a response straight away, then the email has bounced and he has no way to contact Klaus.

Veronica wheels closer so she can look over his shoulder. "Patience isn't your thing, is it?"

His laptop dings, an email appearing in Tristan's inbox.

He almost curses, but then quickly realizes *Undeliverable* isn't in the title.

"Klaus replied," Veronica breathes.

Tristan can't open the email fast enough.

I told you, Dyad isn't even on the radar.

Tristan types out a quick response. Knowing his luck, Klaus's hour at any one location is almost up.

Everyone has a digital footprint. This is urgent.

As he hits send, he notices Veronica chewing her nail. She knows they're either getting closer or they're about to annoy their one lead.

The laptop dings and Tristan hesitates on opening this one. He's not up to another rejection, even from an elderly hacker.

It'll take time.

Veronica whoops, pushing her chair away and gliding across HQ's floor.

"He hasn't found Dyad yet," Tristan points out, even though he's grinning himself.

"Klaus is da man, I can feel it."

Tristan glances back at the laptop, his smile fading as he realizes Klaus needing time could be days. Surely it couldn't take weeks… Veronica sighs as if she realizes they're back to waiting again, too.

She checks her phone. "Still nothing from Jareth or Logan."

"They're undercover," Tristan points out. "I don't think there's much opportunity to text."

She smiles. "True. Maybe we should grab some lunch," she suggests.

"Good idea," Tristan agrees, turning away to hide his face. Not hearing from any of the Zodiacs always makes him nervous, but he's not going to let Veronica know that. This is her brother and boyfriend they're talking about.

His computer dings and he freezes.

Veronica's eyes widen. "No way."

A quick swipe on his laptop confirms that an email's arrived in Tristan's inbox. Just the title makes his heart lurch.

Lucky break.

Quickly opening the email, Tristan sees there's an address, along with a short line afterward.

Stop contacting me.

Tristan grins and Veronica shakes her head as he sends a quick reply.

You da man!

They both head for the door, Veronica pulling out her phone. "You drive, I'll navigate."

The abandoned apartment block that Tristan pulls up across from is one of the dingiest he's ever seen, and he's seen some seedy places. Only a couple of stories high, it squats over the street as if it's constipated. He's pretty sure it's held together with nothing but grime and soot.

"Nice," murmurs Veronica as she climbs out of the car. "Dyad really knows how to live it up."

"Well, it's definitely off the radar." Few people would want to come here.

Tristan walks toward the building and she joins him. If they find Dyad, Tristan doesn't care that he'll have to shower three times a day for the next week just to wash off the gross that has permeated this place.

They both fall silent as they approach the opening that would've once been a door. Even the doorframe is long gone. Tristan and Veronica press themselves against the wall on either side, listening.

All that registers is the sound of traffic a street away and the musty scent of mold. Tristan nods and steps through, Veronica right behind him.

Tense and wired, he isn't sure what he was expecting, but the empty, dirty cavern that he finds himself in is a distinct disappointment.

"It's empty," says Veronica, sounding as bummed as he's feeling. "Maybe he knew we were coming."

"Let's take a look around," Tristan suggests. "See if we can find anything."

They weave their way around saggy mattresses and scattered takeaway containers. Tristan notes that none of it looks recent.

"There's dust on everything," Veronica observes. "And rats have eaten what leftover food there is. No one's been here in a couple of days."

"Yeah, I was just thinking the same thing." Tristan sighs. "We missed him."

Veronica's hands clench. "Well, that sucks."

Tristan stills, angling his head. "Someone's coming."

Veronica spins around. "I can't hear anything." It takes a few seconds, but her eyes widen as she hears it, too.

Cars coming down the street. More than one.

"Do you have sonar or something?" Veronica whispers.

Tristan looks around, spotting a wardrobe at the rear of the building, another doorway beside it. He strides toward it. "My training involved listening for when a pin dropped on carpet."

"Now, that's cool," she says, quickly following him.

He sees that the doorway opens to an alley out the back, a dumpster a few feet away.

"Ew," says Veronica, pinching her nose. "Garbage collection is obviously not on a Tuesday."

"It doesn't seem to be a priority for this area, period," Tristan mutters, covering his own nose.

The sound of running feet has Tristan grabbing Veronica's arm and yanking her out. There's no time to run. They dart behind the dumpster, crouching down.

"Freeze!" shouts a voice from inside the building.

Tristan's muscles coil. That one word means these men aren't here for the ambiance or food. They have guns.

Ignoring the stench that's emanating from the dumpster that's hiding them, Tristan listens hard. He quickly distinguishes several sets of footsteps. They divide up, spreading around the room. They're searching.

Tristan holds six fingers up. They've come out in force.

Veronica frowns, nodding. She loosens up her shoulders, realizing they might be up for a fight.

"Check the back," says a hard voice.

Tristan shifts his weight to the balls of his feet, bracing one hand against the dumpster. Six to two aren't great odds, especially considering these men have guns, but he's had worse.

Gravel crunches as one of them steps through the back door. Tristan keeps his breath slow and steady. Beside him, he's pretty sure Veronica isn't breathing at all.

Long moments stretch out, tightening Tristan's nerves to breaking point.

A second set of footsteps joins the first.

"Jeez, that's disgusting."

"Tell me about it." More gravel crunches. "The alley is clear."

"Sounds good to me."

Their footsteps recede as Veronica lets her breath out. Taking the risk, Tristan peeks around the dumpster. The man is just stepping through the door, but it's all Tristan needed to see.

The man was wearing a suit.

Tristan turns to Veronica, mouthing three letters. "FBI."

She frowns, soundlessly replying. "Nebula?"

Tristan shrugs. He's glad there's no opportunity to talk, or his impulsive side might've just blurted that he's not too sure there's that much of a difference.

Both organizations believe the Zodiacs are a threat.

"He got away," growls a frustrated voice.

"Roll out," orders another.

The footsteps clomp away, heavier now that the agents believe they're alone. And that they've lost their mark.

Tristan and Veronica wait in silence and stench for long minutes, even after the cars have driven away. Once Tristan has counted to a hundred without hearing any other sign of human movement, he straightens.

Veronica groans as she does the same. "This is why you go on about squats, isn't it?"

Tristan shakes his legs out. "That, and they give you a great ass," he says, slapping his backside.

Veronica glances over her shoulder at her own. "Oh, yes, you're right."

They chuckle, but the sound is cut short as they have to draw in deeper breaths. Tristan indicates that it's time for them to do the same as the FBI.

Roll out.

They jog down the alleyway, making sure it's clear when they reach the end. They've just reached the car when Veronica pauses, her hand on the door.

"The agent said whoever they were looking for got away."

Tristan nods, wondering if she realizes the implications of that. Because he's sure they weren't talking about him.

And he doubts those were every day, stodgy, rule-respecting FBI agents.

He'd bet Brielle's next batch of cookies they were Skins.

Which means Chardis wants Dyad.

He opens his door. "Let's get back to HQ. First, we shower. Then, the Zodiacs need to meet."

Because Chardis either wants Dyad because of his ability to crack the key.

Or because Dyad is a Zodiac.

13

ADA

"Where are we going?" Eric asks as he takes the left turn Ada just instructed him to.

Ada grins as they merge onto the highway. "It doesn't matter how many times you ask, I'm not going to tell you. It's a surprise."

Eric's lips thin. "Which is code for 'I don't want to tell you.'"

"Just keep heading to the city," she says, not in the least perturbed. "Let's just say I want to do some shopping."

Eric slides her a glance. "Surely Esther doesn't need anything else? That computer has better security than the Pentagon."

Ada rubs the computer sitting on her lap affectionately. "She really does. But no, it's not for Esther." She glances ahead, seeing the Pizzeria she was keeping an eye out for. "Actually, I wanted a new outfit."

Eric's eyebrows shoot up. "You what?"

"You heard me," she says chirpily. "Just pull over here. Outside the pizza joint." She glances at her watch.

They're right on time.

Still looking surprised, Eric does as he's told. "You never buy clothes. In fact, you'd buy an outfit for Esther before you'd buy one for yourself."

Ada grins, her eyes lighting up. "Someone really needs to take that idea to Shark Tank. They'd be millionaires." She angles her head in thought. "Esther would wear grunge. Lots of black with a red tartan mini-skirt."

Eric glances at the pizzeria. "So what are we doing here? You don't even like pizza."

Looking at her watch again, Ada taps her foot. "They'd better not be late."

Just as she finishes the sentence, a courier van pulls up in front of them. A man gets out, holding a parcel in one hand while checking his clipboard with another. His face is scrunched with concentration as he double checks the paperwork in front of him.

"Give me a sec," Ada says as she hops out of the car.

"Ada—"

But she quickly shuts the door on Eric's question. He'll find out soon enough.

She approaches the delivery guy and signs for the parcel, skipping back to the car. Eric watches her the whole time, curiosity evident in the slight tilt of his head, suspicion evident in the way his fingers drum on the steering wheel. He knows she's up to something.

Ada climbs in and tears open the package, holding the contents. "See? I told you I wanted a new outfit."

"That you ordered online and had delivered to this exact location at this exact time?"

"Yep," she says cheerily. "We've got places to be."

And people to avoid, which is why she needs this disguise.

"Ada—"

"Next stop: the city."

Eric hesitates, his hand on the gear stick. "Where in the city? What for? Why am I even doing this?"

Ada leans over and presses a kiss to his cheek. "Patience, grasshopper."

He sighs as he puts the car into gear. "Man, you're lucky I love you."

Ada doesn't say anything as they pull into traffic. Eric's love is everything to her, and she really is lucky to have it. Which is what makes all these secrets even less okay. She's taking advantage of his faith in her. His desire to make her happy.

She mentally steels herself. She's doing this so they can have answers. So they can have a chance at a normal life.

She pulls out the skirt and jacket she bought. "Now, I just need to get changed."

"What?" Eric squeaks. "Here?"

"I can't go to where we're going dressed like this, can I?" she says, undoing her jeans.

"I wouldn't know," Eric shoots back as he pulls to a stop at a set of lights. "You won't tell me where I'm going."

The lights turn green and Ada uses the opportunity to shimmy out of her jeans. From the corner of her eye, she sees Eric flush red. Although they've always been comfortable around each other, she knows he's doing what she does if she catches a glimpse of his skin.

Trying not to look because it's going to be nothing but torture.

Looking anyway.

Then suffering at the knowledge you can't touch what's so close and deliciously tantalizing, yet impossible to have.

They used to tease each other...until Ada almost fried the both of them when they kissed.

She quickly slips on the skirt, trying to quash the growing

awareness heating up the car. At this rate, they're going to have to turn on the A/C.

Eric unwinds the moment she's modestly covered. It's only then that he does a double take. "What in the world are you wearing?"

It's a fair question. Ada can't remember the last time she wore a skirt, let alone a classy black one like this. In fact, she doesn't think she's ever worn anything remotely like this. She much prefers torn jeans and t-shirts.

"A business skirt." Ada slips on the matching black jacket, buttoning it over her white t-shirt. At least she doesn't have to change her top half. "And a jacket." She notices what street they're on. "Oh, take a right here."

Frowning, Eric takes the turn. He opens his mouth and Ada braces herself to take more evasive maneuvers the moment he notices where they are. She desperately tries to think of a distraction.

Her cell phone dings and a glance at the screen tells her a notification has come in.

Frowning, she reaches into the back seat for Esther. "Someone's snooping around at our last hang out," she tells Eric.

He instantly pulls over into an adjacent parking lot. "Who?"

Ada opens her laptop. "Let's find out."

She logs into the security camera she installed in a corner of the wardrobe, and the dilapidated room appears on her screen. Eric leans over as they see two people walking around.

"A guy and a girl," Eric murmurs. "Why are they snooping around?"

Ada narrows her eyes as she zooms in on the guy. "Tristan Ayers," she breathes.

"Who?"

Ada quickly swipes to a word document she's already created. "Tristan Ayers, also known as Gemini1 on UFO Fanatics. Seventeen. Both parents dead. Lives in a house with another guy, probably having one permanent party. Attends Mirror Point High. Joined our website not long after its inception, but hasn't been very active over the past year or so."

"You've already profiled him?" Eric asks, incredulous, but also looking a little impressed.

"Of course I have. This guy wants to talk to Dyad. In fact, he tried to bait me. I need to know what I'm dealing with." She clicks back on the camera feed. "The question is, what is he doing at our old hangout?"

Eric leans back, his face thoughtful. "You know, if you replied, you'd probably find out."

"I've already told you why I'm not doing that. I need to know what this Tristan wants before I even think of exposing us."

"I know why you're cautious, Ada. It's just that..." He sighs. "I don't think this guy is the enemy."

"You have no way of knowing that." She opens a different document, showing him another profile. "Remember TruthSeeker765? She seemed genuine, so I strung her along—yes, she turned out to be female. She also turned out to be FBI."

Eric frowns. "Oh."

"Yes, oh. And we both know the moment they locate me, even if I leverage some sort of deal, that juvie will be my next hangout. For quite some time."

Dyad has slipped past the defenses of too many large corporations. CEOs and their over-paid lawyers will be clamoring to have her put away for as long as they can.

"Not happening," he growls. "We'll always be together, Ada. No matter what."

"Damned straight." She takes his hand and squeezes it. "Which is why we need to find out what the message says."

They both realized a long time ago that their powers aren't from this world. They can't be. Nothing on Earth can explain what they can do.

There's a flicker of movement on Esther's screen and they both glance back. Tristan and the girl who's with him run past the wardrobe.

"They just left through the back door," says Eric.

"They're about to meet the abominable dumpster," says Ada, her stomach rolling at just the thought of the smell. "They'll be back any second."

Except they don't. Instead, more people enter the area. Six men in suits. And they're all holding guns.

Ada and Eric's clasped hands tighten around each other as they watch the agents sweep the room, two walking past the wardrobe just like Tristan and the girl did. Their handguns wave back and forth, coldly scanning for their target.

Ada.

After several minutes, they realize the place is empty and they leave as stealthily as they arrived. Tristan and the other girl are nowhere to be seen.

Eric flops back in his seat. "They must've traced the car," he breathes.

"You changed the plates, remember?" Ada reassures, even though her heart is hammering. That was a close call. The closest so far.

"We need to disappear for a while," Eric says, a thread of panic in his voice. "We have the money from your last job, it'll be enough for us to drop off the radar for a few weeks."

Ada's own panic flares. "What? No," she almost cries. "We can't, we're too close to back out now."

"That's exactly why they're picking up our trail, Ada. Because we're getting close."

"Please, Eric." She reaches out to him, her hand hovering. "I need to know the truth."

For herself. And for their future.

And she can't do this without him. She's only one half of a whole without Eric.

Eric clasps her hands as he lets out a long breath. "I know I'll regret it, but okay. What's the plan?"

Relief is a tsunami through Ada. She pulls up a smile, trying to make it confident. "I get the code. I decipher the key. Voila."

"And how are you going to do that?"

Ada points to the building that the parking lot they're in adjoins. Three letters are stamped across the front.

F. B. I.

"I'm not waiting for a job offer," she says, equal parts excitement and fear buzzing through her veins. "I'm going to pose as a mail boy. Today."

14

BRIELLE

"I'm here to see Mr. Sinclair. Is he available?"

A tremble shivers down Brielle's spine as she stands in front of the stupidly pretty blonde receptionist, and she can't quite shake it. Her whole body feels like a noodle, and she's not sure if that's from nerves or the anger and hatred she feels toward Cassandra's dad.

She doesn't know how she's going to be able to face him. How she's going to sit in front of him with a polite smile when all she wants to do is use the fighting skills Tristan has taught her to make him hurt.

The receptionist looks up at her, and Brielle can tell she recognizes her from the previous day. "Let me check," the receptionist replies with a guarded tone as she regards her computer screen. "Yes, it appears he has no appointments until one. I'll ask if he's willing to see you."

Brielle opens her mouth to try to stop her, because she was hoping to walk in unannounced—there's no way he will see her now—but it's too late; the receptionist has already pressed the intercom button.

"I have a young lady here to see you," she announces. "A miss…"

"Brielle Pierce," she offers.

"Brielle Pierce," the receptionist parrots.

"Ah, yes, send her in," Cassandra's dad's voice says through the speaker.

"Right away, sir." The living mannequin nods in the direction of the door with his name on it.

"Thank you," Brielle says, then heads toward his office.

She takes a deep breath before turning the knob and opening the door.

"Good morning, Miss Pierce," he welcomes from behind his desk. He glances at his computer screen. "While I am pleased to see you here, shouldn't you be in school?"

Brielle gulps down her storming emotions. "Actually it's fall break, which I'm glad for. I couldn't imagine having to go to school after what happened to my dad. Did you hear that he got arrested?"

He nods, his face adopting a pitying frown. "Yes, I heard about the whole mess with the IRS." His voice is so steady, filled with sympathy, and she can feel the lie even in his tone. "What a terrible thing to happen." He shakes his head, then waves a hand to invite her to sit across from him, which she accepts. "How can I help?"

By admitting what you did and spending the rest of your wretched life in prison, where you belong.

"I was wondering—well, actually hoping—you might know how this could have happened." She's surprised by how steady her own voice is, and how devoid of the anger bubbling beneath her skin.

"I'm sorry to say that I had no idea your dad's company was in such a bad way." *Lie.* "We're usually very careful about which companies we make deals with. I'm surprised we didn't find the issue sooner. It's given us quite a lot of bad press." He attempts a sympathetic pout. "It's never pleasant to find out that someone you trust is capable of bad things. I'm so sorry for you." *Lies!*

Brielle moistens her lips, hiding her clenching fists under the desk. "Actually, I'm certain he's innocent of what they're accusing him of. I believe someone framed him. I was hoping you could possibly help me prove his innocence."

A flicker of suspicion and knowing flashes in his steel eyes, but his seemingly genuine expression doesn't waver. "Due to the bad press I mentioned, I'm incapable of conducting any further business with your dad's company, unfortunately."

The anger rises to the surface, and it's all Brielle can do not let it show on her face.

"But...perhaps I can help you in a different way," he adds, the corners of his lips curling ever so slightly. "If you recall, a while ago I offered you a job as my intern. I'm aware that you interned for Frank as well, so you have the skills required for the position. With Frank, let's say, on leave, I'm sure your family will need some financial assistance, and I'd be glad to offer it in exchange for your work. And, in turn, if you do a good job, I might be inclined to get my hands a bit dirty and investigate any possible fraud on our part."

"You—you want me to come work for you?" *I'd rather peel off my own fingernails with an ice pick.*

"Absolutely. I'm nothing if not philanthropic."

He thinks he's doing her a charity? She contemplates using the penance burn on him, forcing him to face his guilt for all the terrible things he's done and suffer for it. Although she doubts even then he would confess, and she'd expose herself in the process. While it's incredibly tempting, she needs to find her information through other means. At least for now.

She's certain she will one day inflict it on him, but today is not that day.

And, she realizes, maybe by working for him and becoming part of his inner circle, she can find the proof she's after. She also needs to get him out of the office so Cassandra can snoop. Though how Cassandra will manage to get past the warden at the receptionist desk, Brielle has no idea.

"That's a tempting offer." Not a lie. Her stomach growls, she'd been too stressed to eat breakfast before leaving the house, and she's grateful for the audible proof for her next statement. "Excuse me, I didn't eat today. I can't really think straight." She rubs her forehead for show.

"Then let me take you out to lunch and we can discuss the matter further," he offers, looking pleased at her lack of rejection.

"Thank you, that would be nice," she says, inwardly jumping that he took the bait. Who needs lying when subtle suggestion works so much better? And it comes to her so naturally from years of refusing the former.

"Excellent." He stands and gestures for her to precede him from the office. "Jeanie, I'm going out to an early lunch," he tells the receptionist. "Hold all my calls and move my one o-clock to two."

"Yes, sir," she says as they head into the elevator.

Once in the parking lot, Mr. Sinclair invites Brielle into his black Mercedes. She's incredibly uncomfortable at the thought of being alone with him in such confined quarters. The images of the horrible things he's done to women, to Cassandra, that she saw in her visions rush through her mind, and her guts twist in repulsion.

But she's already come this far, and it's the only way to proceed. And if he tries anything, she's confident she could defend herself. She's fought off literally hundreds of Skins, and he's only human.

Hiding her reluctance, she gets into the passenger seat

and quickly texts Cassandra that they're leaving the office before he can get into the driver's seat.

The drive is spent with him asking questions about the work she's done for Frank. She answers them amicably, trying to steer the conversation toward his involvement with Frank, hoping that will trigger a vision that will at least guide her toward knowing how he framed Frank, but he continues to veer back to her experience and goals for the future, making her attempts fruitless.

They arrive at the Asian bistro Cassandra had mentioned, a ritzy, expensive restaurant, and Brielle realizes he's trying to buy her compliance. When they enter, the hostess greets him by name and shows them to a private booth. Once again, Brielle's discomfort at being so close to him makes her skin bristle, and she wants to suggest they sit at a table in the open floor plan but ultimately lets it go. Making him comfortable will be the only way he'll talk.

As soon as they're seated, Mr. Sinclair places an order for drinks and a sushi boat large enough for the two of them, and the waitress nods and leaves.

"How much were you making in your internship with Frank?" he asks once they're alone.

"I wasn't doing it for a wage," she says. "I just wanted to help him."

"The man had you doing all that work for free?" Mr. Sinclair snorts a laugh, and she hates him for thinking Frank was using her when she was the one who volunteered to help and wanted nothing in return. "Well, if you come work for me, your starting salary will be well above minimum wage, after a trial month, of course. How does sixteen dollars an hour sound?"

Yep, he's definitely trying to buy her. But why?

"That sounds very generous," she manages to say, unable to find any other words that don't sound insulted.

"You would be required to be in the office only a few hours a week, after school, of course, and there may be some flexibility to do some of the work from home, at your discretion."

"I'm sure I could make that work," she says, again using as unopinionated words as she can.

"Wonderful. So, what do you say?" He takes a sip of his water to allow her a moment to consider.

"When can I start?"

A smile spreads across Mr. Sinclair's face that she's sure is meant to come across as business-like, but to her, it's only devious. "As a matter of fact, I have a...task that's of the utmost importance for you to start on tomorrow. Are you up for it?"

"What's the task?" she asks, unable to keep the tone of suspicion from seeping into her voice.

"Ah, first things first." He opens his briefcase and pulls out a sheet of paper. "First, I need you to sign this non-disclosure agreement, required for all staff."

She accepts the paper. "Mind if I read it first?"

"I wouldn't respect you if you didn't," he says, nodding.

She scans it over, and basically all it says, in very lengthy business terms, is that she can't share any vital information she learns with any third party. She's not sure how that will affect her when she finds the info she's looking for, but she decides she will figure it out when the time comes. She has no choice but to sign it if she wants to go any further with her investigation.

She signs the document, feeling a little bit like she just signed away her soul to the devil.

With a satisfied smile—every kind of smile looks devious on his steely face—he takes the document and puts it back into his briefcase.

"Now then, on to business." He braids his fingers on the

table. "Your first task will be to deliver a thumb drive to, well, let's call him an associate, who is adept at cracking computer codes. For affiliation reasons I'm sure you'll understand, I cannot conduct the business in person."

She blinks as she translates the clever words he used to sugarcoat the truth. "You want me to take this to a hacker? I'm guessing what you're asking is not entirely legal."

He shushes her, then continues in a lower register. "Let's not worry too much about the semantics. This is your first task as my intern, and I want to treat it as no more and no less. I could have simply hired a bicycle courier, but I need someone I can trust for this. Can I trust you?"

No pitching way in Hell. "I'll get the job done. Can I ask what's on the thumb drive?" She has the right to know if it's anything that will get her or Frank into more trouble.

"Certainly," he says with a shrug. "It's what IT professionals call a key, which basically means it's used to decipher complex codes. I believe my associate has the code."

Just then, the waitress arrives with their sushi boat. They eat in silence, and it's agony for Brielle to maintain a polite façade. She can't stop wondering what code his key might be needed to crack. Surely it couldn't be the one Tristan is trying to crack. A thought jolts through her. Could it have anything to do with Frank? Her urgency to find out makes it hard to eat, so she lets Mr. Sinclair finish off most of the sushi.

"Arrive at the office tomorrow around one, and I will give you the key and the address to take it to," he says.

"Thank you, Mr. Sinclair," she says.

"Please, call me Richard," he invites.

Never in a million years. "Yes, sir." Although even calling him sir makes her guts twist with disgust. He doesn't deserve the respect of that title.

"I have to return to the office, but I have arranged for a

car to pick you up and take you wherever you'd like to go," he says, then rises from the table and makes his exit from the restaurant.

Brielle pulls out her phone.

It picks up after one ring. "Yeah?"

"He's heading back to the office," Brielle tells Cassandra. "You'd better get out of there."

"Ugh, no such luck," Cassandra groans. "Warden Jeanie wouldn't let me in. I didn't get anything."

"Well, I may have," Brielle says. "I'll meet you in fifteen."

JACK

14:23

Jack throws a cup of water in Flanagan's face. The asshole grunts then shakes his head, a moment later trying to surge to his feet. Jack watches in satisfaction as the guy who calls himself his boss realizes he's strapped to a chair.

The same guy who interrogated and tortured Logan.

Flanagan jerks against the tape binding his arms and legs, the chair scraping across the floor. His hand hits the table he's sitting beside, yanking out a curse. Jack smiles, stepping back in the dining area they're in. The FBI safe house where he met Logan to talk to the alien his son captured seemed like the ideal place to have this conversation.

Flanagan's head snaps up, any signs of the tranquilizer Jack and the other Nebula agents used to transport him gone. He registers that the three men who were working with him are also here, just as immobilized as he is. One softly groans as he starts to regain consciousness. Realizing where he is—

Flanagan would know this safe house just as any FBI agent in the area would—his gaze snaps to Jack.

"Release me, and that's an order."

The two Nebula operatives standing behind Jack step forward, but Jack lifts his hand. He intends on having this conversation himself.

He angles his head. "I stopped taking orders from you quite some time ago, Flanagan." He leans forward. "Today, I ask the questions and you answer."

Flanagan's eyelids drop down in a sleepy, defiant expression. "You never did know how to follow orders, Cadbury. It's why I was promoted and you weren't."

Jack resists the urge to punch Flanagan. He's saving his knuckles for when it really counts.

"Why did you interrogate my son?" he demands.

A man groans on Flanagan's right, his head lolling until he's glaring at Jack. Russo—an agent who started in the agency at the same time as Jack three decades ago—glares at him. "Your son is a traitor."

Jack ignores him. Logan is the one person he can trust. He turns back to Flanagan. "Why?"

Flanagan shrugs. "We wanted to see what he knew."

Which means Flanagan may have an inkling that Nebula exists. The fact that he went after Jack's son to get confirmation has fury bubbling through his veins. His palms itch and he clenches them compulsively, noting the way Russo's gaze flickers to them.

Good. They need to know he means business.

Jack turns to Flanagan. "Who is Solomon?"

"A guy in the bible who didn't want a haircut?"

"That's Samson, you idiot." Jack releases all the rage he felt when he saw his son's damaged body as he slams his fist into Flanagan's face. His head snaps to the side with the force, his soft cheek rippling with the impact.

"Where is he?" growls Jack.

Flanagan jiggles his jaw from side to side. "Don't care."

The second strike has pain jolting up Jack's arm and his knuckles throbbing, but he welcomes it. If it's hurting him, then Flanagan has got to be feeling it, too. "Where's the key?"

"I wouldn't be here if I had it," Flanagan sneers through his bloody lips.

Jack's about to hit him again, when Russo's voice reaches him. "You'll beat him and your fist to a pulp, and you still won't have any answers. We won't talk."

Jack spins around to face the man he's known for over three decades. Russo was a mild-mannered agent counting his days down to retirement. He'd plonked his soft ass in a chair at this desk and only got up to eat, use the men's, or go home. Jack leans forward and Russo's face hardens in a way he's never seen before. It's obvious something has changed him.

Russo spits in his face, the globule slapping Jack's cheek and slowly smearing down. Disgust shoots through Jack's gut. He's about to pull back when he stops. A thin, silvery line surrounds Russo's irises.

A thin, silvery line that doesn't belong in any human eye.

That's why Russo is behaving so differently. He's corrupted. Maybe being controlled somehow.

Jack puts his hands on his hips, the motion opening his jacket and exposing his firearm. "You talk or you die," he states simply.

"You won't shoot us," sneers Russo. "You've got too much to lose."

Jack nods. "You're right. That's why I'm going to make it look like an accident."

Flanagan jerks on his bonds. "You don't have the guts, Cadbury."

Jack moves toward him, peering at his face. The same

silver ring surrounds Flanagan's irises.

He draws back, realizing that will make what he has to do a whole lot easier. Taking a step back, he looks at the four men. "A bunch of FBI agents, playing poker. Never realizing there was a gas leak…"

The Nebula agent to Jack's left flicks the knob on the stove and a soft hissing sound fills the room.

"Someone lit a cigarette," Jack says as he places a pack on the table. The deck of cards has already been scattered on it. He takes a step back. "And…boom."

Not one of the FBI agents blinks at the threat. And each and every one of them keeps their mouths tightly shut.

All except for Flanagan. "You're already losing."

"Not from where I'm standing," snaps Jack. "Would anyone like to share what they know about the message?"

The hissing of the gas is all that fills the room.

"Very well." Jack spins on his heel, his agents falling in behind him. He exits through the front door, never once looking back.

Death isn't something he rejoices in. Revenge isn't an emotion that's ever really driven him.

But that was when Jack was dealing with humans.

And whatever he just left behind in that room isn't human.

Jack climbs into his car along with the two Nebula agents. He turns the key and the engine purrs to life. Heading down the driveway and onto the street, he glances in the rear vision mirror.

"Do it."

The explosion is muffled by the car they're encased in, but the flare of flames isn't. It bathes the interior of the car in orange and red, sending grim shadows over their faces.

Jack accelerates away.

He'll find his answers elsewhere.

15

CASSANDRA

C assandra taps her foot impatiently as she sits on a curb in the parking garage of her dad's office. She should have known that Jeanie wouldn't let her in. After everything that happened yesterday, he would've certainly made it clear to Jeanie that his exiled daughter was no longer welcome.

She doesn't even know why she bothered coming. She should be with Logan. He'd called her last night after he'd gotten home and told her about his capture. Though he wouldn't say, she knows his captors had hurt him. She wanted to go to him right then, but he insisted he was fine.

Logan shouldn't even be doing any reconnaissance, seeing as he only just got out of the hospital after surviving a gunshot. He should be lying low, resting, regaining his strength. But telling him to do so is like trying to force a stone to roll uphill. It's not the way he was made. Logan is a man of action, no matter what the personal cost to himself.

"Cassandra," Brielle calls, jogging over to her.

She looks up to see a black sedan driving away from Brielle. Her dad sent her with a private car? He really does want Brielle. But for what?

"So, what happened?" Cassandra asks eagerly, standing up.

"Your dad offered me a job," Brielle replies.

Cassandra blinks hard. "What?"

"He wants me to start tomorrow," Brielle continues.

"A job doing what?"

Brielle furrows her brow. "He says he wants me to be his intern, but the first task he's assigned me sounds very shady. He wants me to deliver some kind of key to a hacker."

"A key? Like, to a house or a car? Why would a hacker need a key?" This does sound very shady indeed.

"No, not that type of key." Brielle shakes her head. "It's a thumb drive with some sort of cipher to crack a code. What do you think it could be for?"

"Whatever it is, it can't be good. Do you have it?"

"No. He said he'll give it to me tomorrow."

They both stand in quiet suspicion for a moment, until the silence is broken by their phones dinging in sync. They pull them out.

It's a group text from Tristan. "We need to meet at HQ asap."

"Let's go," Cassandra says, and they head to her car parked behind a large pillar in the corner so it wouldn't be seen.

When they get to Tristan's, the gang is already there, everyone waiting inside HQ.

Cassandra's eyes immediately find Logan, and her heart aches as she sees the black eye. She runs to him and throws her arm around his neck. He grimaces, and she loosens her admittedly too-firm hold on him.

"Are you okay?" she asks, cupping his face in her hands.

"Just a little banged up, but I'll live," he jokes.

She narrows her eyes. "I should have been the one to go with you. This wouldn't have happened if I was there."

"I'm glad you weren't," he says, his tone softening. "I couldn't bear it if they'd taken you, too. Jareth at least had a cover to keep him protected. You wouldn't have."

"Maybe not, but I would've blasted anyone before they got close enough to lay a finger on you." She bristles, her anger rising. She imagines the sweet satisfaction of torching the man who gave Logan that black eye.

"And you would have outed all of us if you had," he says.

She knows he's right, but what good are her powers if she can't protect the people she cares about, and punish those who threaten them?

Tristan comes into the room, and everyone quietens and gives him their attention. Cassandra isn't done arguing yet, but it can wait. Tristan wouldn't have called them all if it wasn't important.

"Veronica and I were able to find the hacker I was looking for, but the message is too encrypted for him to decipher," Tristan begins right away. "He says it requires a key to decode it, and while we have no idea how to find the key, he turned us in the direction of someone who might. A dark web hacker who calls himself Dyad."

"Wait, did you say key?" Brielle interrupts.

Tristan chances a glance at her, clearly not wanting to meet her eyes. "Yes?"

"I had lunch with Cassandra's dad just now—long story," she adds when he gives her a perplexed look. "He wants to hire me as his intern, and I thought it would be the best way to find out about my dad's arrest and how to find Solomon."

"Your dad's been arrested?" he exclaims.

A shadow falls over her face, and she looks away. "Yeah, like I said, it's a long story."

Tristan frowns, seeming hurt. "Why didn't you tell me?"

"Look, that's not the point right now," she hedges. "He told me he has a key that he wants me to take to a hacker he knows to find out what code it goes to. This has to be our key!"

Tristan's eyes widen. "Do you have it?"

She shakes her head. "He's going to give it to me tomorrow when I officially start working for him."

He crosses his arms over his chest, the flicker of excitement that momentarily flashed in his eyes darkening to suspicion. "Do you think he knows we have the code it goes to?"

"If he did, there's no way he'd hand it over to us," Cassandra says. "My guess is he has no idea what it corresponds to, only that it's important. I just don't understand why he'd have it."

"He must be linked to Chardis somehow," Tristan muses. "We already know he was affiliated with Solomon."

"As soon as I get the key, I'll bring it here first," Brielle says. "Then we can decode the message."

"It's not that simple," Veronica interjects. "According to Klaus, even with the key, it would take a very talented hacker to crack."

"So, we still need to find Dyad." Tristan sighs.

"How do we do that?" Brielle asks, frustration pinching her brow.

A subtle ding cuts through the tense air, and Tristan checks his phone. Then his eyes widen and he holds it closer to his face, the excitement returning. "It's a text from Klaus. He says he's located Dyad's signature at the FBI building."

Cassandra's eyes snap to Logan. He just narrowly escaped the clutches of undercover Skins there. "You're not seriously suggesting we go there. After what happened to Logan and Jareth."

"We have to," Tristan insists. "We need Dyad. We can't decode the message without him."

"Besides, the crooked agents who withheld me have been dealt with," Logan adds.

"That doesn't mean there aren't more of them," Cassandra declares. "If you think I'm letting you walk back into that building, you're insane." She turns to Tristan. "If you insist on following this Dyad person into a trap, then I'm going with you this time. No one else is going to get hurt, not if I can help it."

The others all exchange glances, and no one is willing to argue with Cassandra over this.

"Alright, looks like we have a plan," Tristan says. He looks to Brielle. "I'll let you know once we've found Dyad."

Brielle nods.

Tristan seems like he wants to say more, but now isn't the time for them to get bogged down in their weird emotional issues, and he clearly knows that.

"Come on, Cass," he says, heading for the door.

Before she follows him, she clasps Logan's face and covers his lips with a brief yet passionate kiss. "No more getting into trouble while I'm gone."

"So I should wait to get into trouble until you get back?" Logan winks.

She gives him a warning glare, ignoring his joke.

"I'll be fine. I promise," he says finally. He pecks her forehead, and she turns on her heel to follow Tristan before she can change her mind.

This Dyad had better be worth all the fuss, or there'll be hell to pay.

16

TRISTAN

T ristan pauses at the top of the stairs. "Brielle's dad's been arrested?"

Cassandra turns around, her movements far slower than the race up the stairs had been. "Ah, yeah. His company was put into liquidation."

And now she's working as an intern for Richard?

Tristan frowns. Things are weird between him and Brielle, he knows that. But she's not even telling him what's happening in her life anymore? "How? When?"

Cassandra flushes. "We think my dad had something to do with it. He probably used Frank as the fall guy." She shifts uncomfortably. "Look, I'm not the one who should be telling you this."

She's right. It means he and Brielle aren't even friends anymore. When did that happen?

Tristan turns around. "Give me two secs."

He jogs back down the stairs. He can't leave with things like this between them.

Down in HQ, Logan is nowhere to be seen. Hopefully he's gone into one of the rooms further down the tunnel that have army cots with the vial Tristan gave him. Rest and nanites are what he needs right now.

Jareth and Veronica spin around from the computer they were facing and Jareth frowns. "Is something wrong?"

Tristan shakes his head, his gaze capturing Brielle as she sits by her own computer. "I just wanted to have a quick word with Brielle."

"Oh," breathes Veronica. She leaps to her feet. "I'm going to…ah…brush my hair. Wanna come, Jareth?"

He rolls his eyes at the lame excuse. "Sure. It can get pretty tangled."

They scoot past Tristan, who wants to face-palm. They're making this far more awkward than it needs to be.

Brielle stands up. "Did you need me to come with you?"

"No, we're better off if we don't have too many Zodiacs at the FBI building." He hesitates. He doesn't have much time. Nor is he really sure what he wants to say, but the void between them is feeling so much further than just a few feet. "I was just surprised to hear your dad's in jail."

She chews on her lip. "Things have been busy for both of us," she says quietly, her gaze slipping away. "And I didn't want to worry you."

Except he'll always worry about Brielle. He lov—

Tristan sighs. It's those emotions that are getting in the way. Everything he feels for Brielle can't be, and she knows that. What's more, it's getting in the way of the Zodiacs.

He rubs his temple. "I hate that things are getting so…tense."

Brielle wrings her hands. "Me, too."

But how does he stop his feelings for her? When she said she can't be with him? How does he pretend that doesn't slice him open every time he looks at her?

Tristan straightens. He has to. For Brielle. For the Zodiacs.

He takes a step forward and juts out his hand. "Hi, my name's Tristan. Nice to meet you."

Brielle's brow crinkles for a split second before a smile plays at the edge of her lips. She grips his hand and shakes it. "Hi, Tristan. I'm Brielle." She glances around. "Interesting place you've got here."

"The guy who decorated it really wanted to take the doomsday prepper theme into the next century, hence all the technology."

Brielle's smile grows and a corresponding weight shifts from Tristan's chest. This isn't them together, but if that's all he can get, he'll take it.

She takes another look around. "Well, mission accomplished."

Tristan grins, glad she's going along with this. "I was hoping we could be friends. Maybe save the world together or something?"

Brielle flushes. "I'd like that."

"Awesome," Tristan says, realizing how lame that sounded. Then also realizing they're still holding hands.

He clears his throat as he releases her and steps back. Friends he can do.

He doesn't have a choice.

"I've gotta go, there's a hacker I need to talk to, but make yourself at home," he jokes lightly. "There's canned cheeseburgers in one of the back rooms if you're feeling peckish."

Brielle wrinkles her nose. "Thanks, but I'd have to be pretty hungry to eat that."

Tristan shrugs. "Good call. I tried some last week and I'm not sure I've digested them yet."

Brielle takes a small step forward. "Thanks, Tristan."

He pauses, his heart responding to the soft note in her voice. He's missed talking and joking with Brielle like this.

He's missed…her. Surely he can do this if it means he'll have that back again.

He smiles. "That's what friends are for."

He turns and lopes up the stairs, finding that Cassandra is at the top, waiting. He tries to find the smile again, but it's nowhere to be found.

Friends he can do, he tells himself.

Friends is what's best for everyone.

She raises her brows. "All sorted?"

"Sure," he says dryly. How can anything be okay when he feels like this?

Cassandra juts out a hip. "You know it's obvious that you care for her. I don't know why you don't just"—she waves her hand in the air as if she's trying to bring every lovesick couple in the world together—"find a way to make it work."

"I tried," he snaps, noting the shock on Cassandra's face. "This"—he waves his hand around in the same way she just did—"is Brielle's choice."

Tristan strides past her, pretending there isn't a bitter taste in his mouth.

Friends is the best he can hope for.

17

BRIELLE

Brielle moves up in the line behind Veronica, who's now being served by Madge.

With Tristan and Cassandra out on the mission to locate this elusive hacker, Veronica suggested the rest of them go to Creamy Dreams to help them unwind while they wait. Brielle was grateful for the opportunity, because she knew that she'd spend the entire time worrying.

After Logan and Jareth had been apprehended and roughly interrogated—to sugarcoat it—Brielle was far from thrilled that her ex-boyfriend and best friend were going to the same building. If Logan's own reputation as the son of one of their own wasn't enough to protect him from such a thing, then Tristan, someone previously wanted for terrorism, didn't stand a chance.

But she can't think like that. Tristan was the most capable of all of them, and he had Cassandra with him, who could blow up the entire building if she wanted to.

"Where's your adorable friend?" Madge asks, making Veronica giggle.

"On a top secret mission," Veronica says in an exaggerat-edly hushed voice.

Brielle looks away, as if to avoid the topic of Tristan. Her wandering eyes land on the "Help Wanted" sign taped to the inside of the glass door. She stares at it for a long, blank moment.

"What can I get you today, dear?" she hears Madge ask her.

Brielle turns to her. "Actually, can I get an application form?"

Madge's green eyes light up. "Absolutely!" She rifles under the counter for a second, then hands Brielle the form and a pen over the buffet shield. "You're the second person to request one today. It'll be nice to have some familiar faces on the other side of the counter."

"Thanks." Brielle accepts the application and takes it to the table her friends have convened at.

"You go up there for a fro-yo and come back with a piece of paper," Jareth states, poking his spoon at the curled point of his frozen concoction. "What's up with that?"

"I'm not really in the mood for sweets," Brielle says with a shrug. "And I could really use a part-time job."

"Didn't you say Cassandra's dad just hired you as an intern?" Veronica asks around a mouthful of fruit.

"Yes, but I won't start to get paid for that until I've been there a month, and I don't intend to stick around that long." *At least, I hope it won't take that long to clear Frank's name.* "And I could really use the money now." Frank's going to need a lawyer, and even if Bea won't let her contribute to those funds, she can at least make money for her own necessities. She won't just sit on the sidelines and be a burden.

She fills out the form, grateful to have something this trivial to distract her from her worries for even a brief moment. Madge had said there was someone else who applied for the job. She wonders who they might be, or if she knows them. And she hopes that whoever they are doesn't beat her to the punch. But if they do, she'll apply somewhere else. Going on a job hunt sounds like the perfect thing to do right now. The perfect way to be helpful.

Once she has everything filled out, she goes back to the counter. A boy is talking to Madge, so Brielle waits her turn. To her surprise, the boy hands the same piece of paper to Madge. He's applying for the job, too?

"Wow, two applicants in one day, at the same time even!" Madge exclaims, seeing Brielle waiting for her. She reaches out a hand to accept Brielle's application as well, and she hands it over.

The boy turns to look at his competition, and Brielle attempts a smile that falters when she sees his face. With raven black hair that frames the top of his head like a crown of feathers and penetrating amber eyes that shimmer like rubies, he's the second hottest guy she's ever seen—Tristan forever holding the title of first place. But this guy's allure isn't the boy-next-door charm like Tristan's. This guy looks like a bad boy, even more so when the right corner of his lip curls upward as he appraises her.

"So, I guess we're applying for the same job," he says, eyes scanning her up and down. His voice is deep and just as russet as his eyes.

"I guess we are," she says.

"Lucky for you both that we have two openings," Madge says, flaring her brows and smiling at them like she's a match-maker. "I'll just take these to the boss. Hang tight, you two." She disappears into the back room.

"I'm Kerrim." He offers a hand.

Brielle accepts his invitation, blushing as their hands meet and his engulfs hers with a heat she wasn't expecting.

Like it could burn her...and she doesn't mind getting burned...

"I'm Brielle," she says. She realizes he's still holding her hand, and when she pulls it away, she suddenly feels very exposed and uses the same hand to tuck her hair behind her ear. "Um, I haven't seen you around here before. Do you go to Mirror Point High?"

Of course, he doesn't. There's no way she wouldn't have noticed him before.

"Nah, I just moved here," he says, then leans closer. "And I graduated two years ago." He winks.

That would make him nineteen or twenty. Somehow, that only makes him more interesting.

She hugs herself, not knowing what else to do with her hands. "What brings you to our sleepy little town?"

"My father moved to the city to do some research for a future business venture," he says, his eyes never leaving hers. This kind of keen attention makes her stomach feel like jelly. "There weren't any openings for me there, so I figured I'd look here. I'm glad I did." He bites his lower lip as he smiles, and her insides melt even further.

She makes a nervous laugh, forcing herself to look away.

"Good news!" Madge returns from the back room, practically skipping. "You've both got the job!" She hands them each a white t-shirt with the Creamy Dreams logo on it. "You start tomorrow. Be here at eight, sharp."

Brielle takes her shirt, a little stunned at how easily this all worked out. And at the fact that she'll now be working alongside this very attractive guy.

Kerrim hangs his shirt over his shoulder, beaming at her. "Looks like we're going to be coworkers."

"Yep," is all she can say.

"Since we're going to be seeing a lot of each other, how about you let me take you out to a movie?" he arches one of his thick dark eyebrows in a daring expression that looks devilishly handsome.

"Uh…" she stammers. Is he seriously asking her out? After they just met?

Tristan's face flashes in her mind. Tristan, who's currently staking out the FBI HQ in search of some mysterious hacker, a potentially dangerous task. Even considering the offer makes her somehow feel like she's cheating on him.

Only, they're not together. They can never be.

And if she ever hopes to get over Tristan, she needs to move on.

"Yeah, okay," she says finally.

"Yay!" Madge claps her hands.

Brielle's cheeks burn at the applause from her unwanted audience, and she shirks away from Madge's loud voice.

Kerrim chuckles, then gives Brielle his phone. "Put your number in, and I'll call you to set up a time."

Entering her digits as fast as she can, she gives him his phone back, eager to escape Madge's attention.

"Sweet," Kerrim says, looking up from her saved number on his phone. "Talk to you soon."

Blushing furiously, she retreats back to her table of friends, wishing she could just disappear.

"O-M-G, that guy was super hot," Veronica whispers as Brielle sits down.

Brielle purses her lips in embarrassment. "Apparently, I have a date with him."

18

ADA

A da straightens her pencil line skirt, still not quite believing Eric let her do this. It had taken some fast talking and a gazillion promises that she was going to be quick, but in the end, he'd agreed.

Maybe more like resigned himself that he wasn't going to win.

Actually, he almost looked defeated.

Ada straightens her shoulders, shoving a dose of resolve down her spine. She's doing this for them. Without answers, they'll never be able to move forward.

The FBI foyer is large and shiny, the emblem stamped on the marble floor. Ada adjusts her jacket so the fake pass she had made is sitting over the top of her breast pocket. She's about to find out whether her forging and coding skills are up to scratch.

Reaching the elevators, she smiles at a woman in a sharp looking suit beside her and nods politely. The woman's lips barely twitch before she looks away. Good, Ada thinks. Busy people are distracted people. They won't look too closely at the new face on the block.

The elevator dings and they step in. Ada's nerves feel tight and brittle as the narrow walls of the elevator close in. She promised Eric she'd be in and out in twenty minutes—one of the conditions that he finally capitulated under. The less time she's here, the less chance of getting caught.

Except, she has to get in, first.

The woman presses the button for the third floor and swipes her pass. Ada chooses the fifth, mirroring the movements as she swipes her own. She has to consciously make sure she breathes. This is the moment she didn't mention to Eric. If her pass fails, she's trapped in an elevator. In an FBI building. With a fake ID.

There's no way that can end well, Dyad or no Dyad.

The number five button lights up, and Ada's knees go weak with relief as the elevator smoothly ascends. It worked. She's on her way to the fifth floor. On her way to answers.

All she needs is to find a way to connect to the FBI servers and she should have what she needs. To do that, Ada chose a mid-level FBI agent to target. Not too high up the food chain to be too important, but also with enough years under his belt to have some level of responsibility. She needs an agent who would be given the more high priority cases and would know about the code.

Jack Cadbury turned out to be that agent. Associated with the FBI for over thirty years, he rocketed up the chain of command only to stagnate at his current level for the past ten. A widower, he has two kids, one who seems to have followed in his father's footsteps. With his lean frame and balding head, he looks like an agent who failed to kiss the right asses and has been relegated to doing what he does best —crack cases like the Triple Murderer.

The chances of him knowing about the code are high.

The woman exits without glancing at Ada. The moment the doors close, she riffles through the satchel over her shoulder, pulling out several envelopes. "A mail boy's gotta have mail," she quips. Adjusting her jacket again so her pass is visible, she waits for the elevator doors to open.

They slide apart with a soft *ding*. She's here.

Heart thumping against her ribs, Ada finds herself in an open area filled with cubicles, just like she expected. She pointed out to Eric that she's studied the floorplan until she could just about walk through this place with her eyes closed. Taking a sharp left, she heads for the offices that line the corridor she finds herself in.

Jack Cadbury's is the fifth on the left.

People move around, coffee cups in hand, generally paying little attention to her. She keeps her head down, sorting through the half-dozen envelopes as she walks like she's supposed to be here. The sounds of fingers clacking on keyboards and phones ringing float around her. Everyone's busy. Breathe, she tells herself. So far, so good.

She reaches Cadbury's office and knocks.

"He's out on a case," someone says behind her.

Ada jumps, her heart lurching painfully as she spins around. An older woman is eyeballing her as she pushes her glasses further up her nose. Ada smiles. "Oh, that's too bad." She flaps the envelopes in her hand. "HR wanted these to him ASAP."

The woman's eyebrows shoot up. "He's already getting the promotion?"

Ada shrugs. "No idea. I'm just the messenger." She smiles brightly. "I'll just pop them on his desk and he can read the good news when he gets back."

The woman frowns, glancing at Ada's pass. "HR sure works quick. Flanagan's funeral hasn't even been announced."

Ada wrinkles her nose. "You know these big agencies. They like to be efficient."

The woman nods and quickly spins on her heel. "It appears so," she mutters, walking away.

Not wasting any time, Ada swipes her pass and enters the office, shutting the door behind her. She lets out a breath. "That was close."

She glances around, noting the spartan décor and stack of takeaway coffee cups in the wastepaper basket. "Well, Jack. It looks like you're the fave to fill poor ol' Flanagan's boots," she murmurs. From what she read about Jack, it seems like it's a promotion that's long overdue.

Dropping the empty envelopes on the desk, Ada takes a seat. She pulls out Esther and quickly connects her to the desktop computer in front of her. "Time to work your magic, girl."

Esther's screen lights up, as does Jack's computer. A login page with the FBI logo appears, a cursor flashing in the little white box. A few taps on Esther's keyboard and the hacking process begins. Her screen turns black as code starts to stream across it. Without learning Jack's password, Ada won't be getting very far.

She yanks on her sleeves as she waits impatiently, chafing at the formal attire. She can't afford for this to take too long. She wouldn't put it past Eric to storm the place if she's ten seconds late, quite likely ending them both in jail.

Esther dings and Ada leaps a little in her seat. She's more nervous than she realized. But what she sees has her smiling.

Password: *KitKatisNestle.*

Her eyebrows shoot up. "Kinda funny coming from a guy called Cadbury," she murmurs. "Isn't that a chocolate brand somewhere?"

Conscious that the clock on the wall is glaring at her, Ada goes to work. She heads straight to Jack's recently opened files. If he's been working on anything to do with the key, that's where the information will be.

The first folder to come up is labelled Project Solomon. She double clicks on it, deciding to give it a cursory glance. The FBI is fond of naming their task forces with weird labels.

An image of a good looking middle-aged man with silver at his temples comes up. A lawyer according to his bio. A lawyer who the FBI are interested in tracking but haven't been able to. Actually, there are almost two pages of notes outlining their failed attempts to locate him.

"That's not going to help your chances of promotion, Jack," says Ada.

She's just about to close it when she sees the latest file note.

Believed to have the key.

"Holy crap," she breathes.

Excitement tingles down her spine. There's only one key the FBI would be talking about. The key to the code that came through the wormhole.

Working quickly, she transfers the files to her secure remote server and shuts Esther down. There will be time to look more closely at what she found when she gets back. Right now, her twenty minutes are just about up. Eric will be waiting for her in the loading dock.

Tucking her laptop back into her bag, Ada grabs the envelopes and shoves those in, too. "Sorry, Jack," she murmurs as she heads to the door. Hopefully, he'll get the promotion without finding Solomon.

Because Ada has every intention of finding the lawyer first.

Leaving the office, she hurries down the corridor. She's just turned the corner when she almost crashes into the woman who spoke to her when Ada first arrived.

"Sorry," Ada flushes. "Mail to deliver and all that."

The woman's brow crinkles. "I thought you were just dropping off the letters and going."

ADA   113

Dammit. She's noticed that Ada's been here longer than that. Ada pulls up a megawatt smile. "I did. I had a couple more deliveries to make on this floor." She keeps walking toward the elevator as if she has places to be.

She does. Anywhere but here.

The woman's face clears. "Oh. Who?"

Ada's pulse lurches. She didn't bother looking up any other names on this floor. She shrugs. "Agent Something-Or-Other. I deliver so many letters, they all blur." She presses the button for the elevator. "Anyway, gotta go. HR's really riding my ass to get all their internal mail out." She presses the button again, this time a little harder. "Maybe everyone's getting a pay rise or something," she adds cheerily.

Come on. Come on, she begs silently. She needs this elevator.

The woman pulls up a smile as her posture relaxes. "That would be nice..." she lifts her brows and glances at Ada's pass.

Ada raises it to show her photo on it. "Erica. Erica Heart," she says cheerily.

The elevator dings and the doors open, unwinding a little of the tension in her chest. She waves at the woman as she steps in, relieved to see she's still smiling.

The doors close and Ada sags against the metal wall. That was close. She pats Esther in her bag. "Maybe we don't tell Eric about that part."

Pressing the button for the first floor of the parking lot, Ada tries to get her pulse under control. She tells herself it's the excitement of finding out about Solomon and the key, but the way she's watching the buttons count her descent tells her she's lying to herself.

Fear, pure and simple, is powering through her body. It's pointing out what a risk she took coming here. It's reminding her what's at stake if she doesn't get out.

The first floor of the parking lot can't come fast enough, and Ada slips through the doors the moment they're wide enough. The loading dock is on the other side.

She's just about to break into a run when she registers movement from behind one of the cars. A suited agent steps out, gun drawn.

Crap.

Her eyes widen when another agent steps from behind a concrete pillar. Then another from behind a minivan. Four more break away from the shadows and join the others in making a semi-circle around her.

The woman from the fifth floor is one of them. She lifts her gun another inch. "I checked our databases. There's no Erica Heart who works here."

Ada slowly lifts her hands, a bead of sweat zigzagging down her spine. "I don't want any trouble."

"Neither do we," says the agent. "But we do want some answers. Which is why I want you to put your bag down on the ground."

Like hell I will, Ada snarls in her mind. Esther is her best friend. She'd never abandon her like that.

"Then," the female agent continues, "I want you to turn around and place your hands on the wall. Real slow."

Ada sighs. "Before I do, I just wanted you to know the elevator was doing some weird stuff on the way down. I think it might be an electrical fault."

The woman narrows her eyes. "Now."

Ada takes a step back, keeping her hands held high. She draws in a deep breath, feeling the familiar tingle in her palms. Mentally, she apologizes to the agents surrounding her. But she can't afford to get captured. Not when she could finally have some answers for what she's about to do.

The tingle spreads, dancing over her skin. Energy thrums and multiplies as it draws power from the very air around her. Her body heats and cools all at once, her hair beginning to crackle.

The female agent frowns. "Get down. Now!"

Ada almost smiles. There are few times she gets to enjoy her powers. To feel so alive, to let the energy that demands to be acknowledged be free. Her whole body is a livewire right now.

All she has to do is let it go.

Spears of lightning arc out, splitting and dividing as they race through the air. The bolts of electricity find each of the agents simultaneously, jolting and dividing over their chests.

They all drop to the floor, bodies convulsing.

Ada instantly contracts the energy back in, feeling the electricity absorb and diffuse throughout her extremities. She glances at the agents, unconscious and limbs twitching.

"Sorry," she murmurs.

Freedom streaks through her in the same way the electricity just did. She did it. She's free! She takes two steps forward only to freeze. Two people are standing several feet away. Their faces tell her they just saw everything.

And one of them is Tristan Ayers.

19

TRISTAN

T ristan takes in the red-haired livewire in front of him, who looks like a flighty gazelle. He's frozen to the spot in shock, just like Cassandra. In fact, the only people moving are the FBI agents still twitching on the ground.

And yet, elation and excitement are leapfrogging inside him, powered by two realizations.

He has no doubt he's looking at Dyad.

And he just discovered she's the next Zodiac.

He takes a step forward, Cassandra instantly shadowing him. "Hello, Dyad."

The girl flicks her flaming curls over her shoulder, gaze dancing around the parking lot. "Let me pass."

Tristan raises his hands to show he's not a threat. "I just want to talk."

"No thanks." She lifts her own hands and Tristan half expects little bolts to leap between her fingers. "Step back."

But he holds his ground. "We don't mean any harm. In fact, I'm pretty sure you're one of us."

Dyad frowns. "How do I know you don't work for them?" She points to the unconscious agents.

"No need to get insulting," huffs Cassandra. "We have standards, thank you very much."

Tristan lowers his hands and unwinds his body. He can tell that Dyad is wired with more than just the energy she can command. The girl just zapped a bunch of FBI agents, which suggests she was desperate.

And scared.

"Look," he says. He doesn't like being in this building any more than she would. "Is there somewhere we could go to talk? Somewhere public, if that's what would make you comfortable?"

"What would make me comfortable is you backing the hell up," she snarls. "And letting me pass."

Suddenly, Tristan realizes why Dyad is so involved with UFOFanatics. She knows she has powers. And she's started to guess at their origins.

He angles his head. "I have the code, by the way. We could really use your help in cracking it."

Cassandra nods. "It's vitally important that we do."

Dyad's gaze flickers around the parking lot. She's looking for a way out. "I'll break the code, but I have no intention of telling you what it says."

Tristan hovers on the balls of his feet, unsure whether to keep giving her space, or move in closer. He needs her to see they're on the same side.

He indicates to the unconscious agents. "I can explain how you did that."

The young woman hesitates. "A bit of static electricity?"

Tristan grins, already liking her sense of humor. "Yeah. The small amount of voltage you needed to knock out six FBI agents. You don't get that from rubbing your feet on carpet, you know."

"And?" Dyad asks, jutting out a hip.

Tristan draws in a steadying breath. "You're a Zodiac Guardian. An alien sent to Earth to protect you from evil."

"There are twelve of us," adds Cassandra. "We've been looking for the others."

Dyad stares at them, blinking.

The sound of a cell phone vibrating slips through the heavy silence. Dyad stiffens, and Tristan realizes it's hers. Someone is trying to get hold of her.

"I don't have time for these fairytales," she mutters.

Before Tristan can say any more, Dyad spins on her heel and runs. She steps right past the elevators and yanks open the door to the fire escape, disappearing through it.

Tristan and Cassandra bolt after her. The door has just shut when he grabs the handle. An electric jolt spears up his arm, and he instantly retracts it. His heart is all of a sudden thundering in his chest.

"Pitch," he growls. "She's electrified the handle."

"It shouldn't last long," Cassandra says, frustration pulling down her brow. "Then we can go after her."

But Tristan shakes his head, aftershocks dancing up and down his nerves. "She'll be long gone." Someone like Dyad would've had their escape plan carefully considered, even for when something goes wrong. "Plus, I think we need to give her time to think about what we said."

Cassandra huffs as she crosses her arms over her chest. "Time isn't something we have a lot of."

Tristan nudges her with his shoulder. "Not everyone was as excited to hear the explanation for their powers as you were."

Her lips tip up. "That's because my powers are cool."

Dyad's look pretty impressive, too. Tristan turns around and heads back to his car, Cassandra following. "We'll use the time we have to find out everything we can about Dyad."

As they make their way through the parking lot, Tristan allows everything that just happened to sink in.

They've found another Zodiac. One who has the power to harness electricity. Once she joins the team, they'll be at six. That's half of them.

He almost misses a step as he realizes what that means.

This girl could be his Gemini soulmate.

20

BRIELLE

What are you doing tomorrow after work?

Brielle gets the text from Kerrim as soon as they leave Creamy Dreams to head back to Tristan's house—this guy doesn't waste any time. And she can't help but stare at it with burning cheeks as she sits in HQ, waiting for Tristan and Cassandra to come back.

A totally gorgeous new stranger wants to take her out. No secret agenda like Tristan had when they first met. He's not hoping she's some alien princess or his destined soul mate. He just has genuine interest in her. It's both flattering and humbling at the same time. Maybe Tristan isn't her only option in the entire world. Just because he was her first love doesn't mean he's her last. Not that she expects to fall in love with dreamy Kerrim, but his entrance in her life is a nice reminder that there are other fish in the sea.

And yet, she still feels bad for even looking at this text, and certainly for feeling butterflies over it. She and Tristan just broke up, and only hours ago became friends again. She can't help but feel like she's slapping him in the face for considering someone else so quickly.

Then again, even when she and Tristan were making out, she knew for a fact he was considering someone else. Everyone else. Always searching for some perfect match he may never find. She deserves to find lasting happiness with someone else since she knows she could never have that with Tristan.

Just as she decides to reply to Kerrim's text, Tristan and Cassandra enter HQ. They both looked flushed and excited.

"So, did you find Dyad?" Logan is the first to ask, eagerly opening his arms to Cassandra.

She runs into them, pecks his cheek and says, "You bet we did! It was amazing!"

"What happened?" Brielle asks, stuffing her phone into her pocket and leaning on the edge of her seat.

Tristan perches against the desk, as animated as she's ever seen him. "We'd just parked in the parking garage and were about to head into the building, and just as this fiery redhead came out of the elevator, all these feds jumped out to stop her—"

"They held guns up at her, and she blasted them with electricity!" Cassandra interrupts, too giddy to help herself.

"Wait, what do you mean? She had a taser or something?" Jareth asks, crossing his arms and frowning in confusion.

"No, the bolts came out of her fingertips!" Tristan exclaims.

Brielle jumps off the seat. "Are you trying to tell us she's the next Zodiac?"

"That's exactly what I'm telling you." Tristan's eyes are on fire with hope, and seeing that spark casts a shadow on Brielle's excitement. If she's a new Zodiac, then she could be...

"Not only that, she's Dyad," Cassandra adds. "All this time, the person we've been looking for to crack this code has been the next member of our team! And her powers are almost as awesome as mine." She bobbles her head and smiles, making Brielle roll her eyes indulgently.

"Wow, must have been some light show," Veronica says. "I would have paid to see that."

"So where is she? Did you bring her back?" Jareth asks, looking into the hall as if she might pop out.

Tristan's wide open grin flattens a little. "No, she ran away as soon as we confronted her and told her who we are, who she is."

"And you didn't chase her down?" Veronica accuses, hands on her curvy hips.

"Not that we could have if we tried, but also, she'll need time to come around," Tristan explains. "Not a single one of us, except for Cassandra, welcomed the news with open arms."

"Yeah, that's true," Jareth says, and he and Logan nod.

"So, what happens now?" Veronica asks with a pouty frown. "We just wait for her to come to us? What if she never does?"

"All we can do is have faith." Tristan sighs. "I've put up a post on UFOFanatics offering her answers. I have to believe that, at the very least, she'll come to us when she's ready to hear them. Then we just have to try to convince her that she's one of us, and that she needs us as much as we need her."

The room is quiet for a moment as everyone thinks about this. A question is burning inside Brielle's heart, and finally the scorch is too much for her to keep it in any longer.

"Which Zodiac do you think she is?" she asks, her voice cracking.

Tristan meets her gaze, and his eyes answer the question as his mouth stays closed. When he does open it to say something, a red light flashes on the ceiling, and he jumps away from the desk.

"There's someone here." He spins around to look at the monitor that shows the camera feeds around the house. "There's a guy at the front door." Just then, the ring of the doorbell echoes into HQ.

All the guys in the room stiffen, on high alert.

"Who is he?" Logan asks, looking from Tristan to Jareth.

Tristan and Jareth both shake their heads.

"Tristan Ayers," says a strong male voice through the camera feed. "I'm here on Dyad's behalf."

That has Tristan's brows jumping into his hairline. Without hesitation, he strides out of the room and up the stairs.

Everyone exchanges glances, bracing themselves in case this is a trap. They wait as Tristan talks to the guy on the front step, Brielle holding her breath and straining to hear the words they're saying through the feed, but she can't make them out.

A minute later, Tristan looks up at the camera and waves for them all to join him as he lets the guy into the living room. One by one, they all file up the stairs, eager to know what this is about.

"You're not Dyad," Cassandra declares as they enter the wide space, narrowing her eyes suspiciously at him.

"No, I'm her...partner." He puts up his hands in a defensive gesture and shakes his head. "Look, she told me what happened at the FBI office, what you told her. I tried to get her to come here and confront you, but she wouldn't. So I have."

"How did you find me?" Tristan asks, his expression open but guarded.

The blond guy gives him a sidelong glance. "Dyad is a wanted computer hacker. She's always known where to find you."

Tristan frowns and shrugs. "Fair enough. But why have you come to confront us?"

The guy furrows his brow, debating his words before he says them. "Ada—Dyad—and I, have always been different. You saw first hand what she can do. I have similar...interests. If you truly are who you say you are, and you truly do have the...interests that we do, I think we can help each other."

Tristan casts a questioning glance over all of them, his eyes finally falling on Brielle. Judging by the lack of her lie detector going off, Brielle nods.

"Can you show us what your *interests* are?" Tristan asks with a measured tone.

The blond guy raises an eyebrow. "I'm not so sure you want me to do that."

"How can we be sure you're being truthful without proof?" Jareth asks, making the guy turn to look at him. "A few of us saw proof of your friend. I'm sorry to say we need that from you, too."

The blond looks to Tristan, who nods once.

"Okay, but remember, *you* asked for it," the blond says. He scrunches his face. "You might want to brace yourself."

Tristan cocks his head. "Okay..."

The blond sighs, then focuses a glare on Tristan. For a split second, nothing happens. Brielle isn't sure the guy is doing anything, other than looking very inappropriately like he's straining to push the biggest bowel movement ever.

But soon, Tristan lets out a groan and crumples to his feet, curling up in the fetal position.

"Tristan!" Brielle instinctively rushes to his side. She snaps her head at the blond. "Stop it! Stop it!"

The other Zodiacs rush in, fists raised, but the blond raises his hands in the same defensive stance and backs away, and Tristan's writhing comes to an immediate halt.

In seconds, Tristan climbs back to his feet, staring at the

blond guy with wide, incredulous eyes. "That was *excruciating!* And incredible."

The blond wrinkles his nose. "I'm sorry, but I did warn you, and you did ask for it."

"I did," Tristan agrees, panting. He hunches over and catches his breath, holding himself up with his hands on his knees. He looks up at the blond. "You—you can inflict pain at will?"

The guy nods. "Or relieve it." He looks to the others. "What can you do?"

Jareth steps forward, holds out his hand, and a beautiful daisy forms in his hands. Then he waves his hand, and the daisy dissipates.

Then Cassandra holds up her hand and ignites a fireball within it. "You ever do that again, and you *will* get burned."

The guy chuckles. "I come in peace, I swear."

The fireball evaporates, and Cassandra puts her arms back in their crossed position over her chest. Logan puts a comforting hand on her shoulder and takes a step closer. "I can sense and amplify emotions, and I can tell you're very on edge and uncertain right now."

The guy touches his nose with the tip of his index finger. "Right on the nose." Then he looks to Brielle. "And you?"

She clears her throat. "I can sense lies."

"And see visions of a person's past if they're lying," Tristan adds. "And, in dire circumstances, make someone feel extreme guilt over bad things they've done to the point of intense agony." He looks at Brielle. "You always sell yourself short." He winks, and she looks bashfully away.

"And you, the infamous Tristan Ayers?" asks the blond, squaring his shoulders as he faces Tristan. "What's your special talent?"

"So far, I get visions of the future," Tristan answers confidently. "But when I find my match, I'll be able to unleash a power I can't even imagine yet."

The blond looks at Tristan for a moment, then tips his head in acceptance. "Fair enough." He looks at Veronica, waiting.

"Oh, me? Nope, I'm just a lowly human," she says. "I'm dating this guy"—she points a thumb at Jareth—"and I'm this guy's sister"—she points at Logan. "Apparently, he was adopted," she adds in a loud whisper blocked by the back of her hand.

The guy nods. "So…you told Ada that you're all…aliens?"

"Yes," Tristan says firmly. "And so are you and…Ada. Sorry, what's your name again?"

"Oh, right," the guy says, shaking his head. "I'm Eric." He waves, a bit awkwardly.

Despite the fact that he just caused Tristan incredible pain just by willing it, Brielle both likes and trusts Eric. He's the kind of person she doesn't even need her lie detection for. He wears his heart and mind on his sleeve, in his facial expressions. He's the kind of person who not only doesn't need to lie, but also doesn't want to, and that's rare.

"So, what makes you so sure that we're all aliens?" Eric asks, cocking his head slightly and regarding all of them.

"Well, I suspect Ada already thought that or she wouldn't be so big on the UFOFanatics chat," Tristan prefaces. "But the man who raised me was on the Gemini Space Station when our enemy attacked, when we were all sent in pods to Earth. He taught me everything he knew, and because of our enemy, he died, alongside the woman who raised me like a mother."

Eric swallows, hesitating for a moment. "And…who is our enemy?"

"A being called Chardis." Tristan's jaw clenches. "He—or *it* —is living dark matter, and its sole goal is to conquer the

Universe. It can infect any living person, possessing them like a parasite. We call the infected Skins. They can be anyone, anywhere, so we always have to be on our guard."

"Like the FBI agents who recently held Logan and me under interrogation," Jareth adds behind gritted teeth.

Eric looks to Logan, who only nods darkly, and Cassandra holds him tighter.

"If we are what you claim, why were we all sent to Earth?" Eric asks. "If we're aliens, what makes the lot of us so special compared to the rest?"

Tristan sighs, and Brielle imagines he must be tired of reciting the same spew over and over. So she steps up and speaks for him. "The Universe is divided into twelve sectors, each governed by a Zodiac sign, at least the way humans see it. Each sector has one special guardian that protects it, which we call the Zodiac Guardians, and each guardian is gifted with special powers to protect that sector. Each of us, and"—she counts on her fingers—"six others are those special guardians."

Eric considers this for a moment, then frowns. "Wait, that would make thirteen. Aren't there only twelve Zodiac signs?"

Tristan sighs again. "There are two Gemini Guardians. Twin sign, twin guardians. I'm the first. Still missing the second."

Brielle's heart pangs at his remark, and at the twinge of hope she hears at the end of it. Like his search might be over…

Eric gives Tristan a long, scrutinizing look. "And you really believe Ada and I are the next two Guardians?"

"Do you have any other explanation for your powers?" Tristan counters. "Because, if so, I'd love to hear it."

Eric looks down and shakes his head. Then his head pops up. "How can we know for sure?"

"There's a sort of *test*," Tristan hedges. "If you can get Ada here, we can test you both at the same time, see which Zodiac you both belong to. Then you'll both have your proof. You'll both know you belong with us."

A hope as bright as the morning sun ignites Eric's sky blue eyes, and Brielle can swear she hears him stop breathing. "I'll do whatever it takes to get her to come, even if I have to drag her here myself."

This brings a smile to Tristan's lips, and Brielle doesn't like the crook of that smile. "We all look forward to it, and to welcoming you both to our team."

Eric shoots out a strong hand, and Tristan shakes it. "I'll be in touch soon." Then he darts out of the house with determination.

The room is quiet for a moment as they all process what just happened.

"Did we really just find *two* Zodiacs in one day?" Cassandra asks.

"I think we did," Tristan answers.

And one of them might be the Gemini Twin.

21

ADA

"Why tomorrow?" Eric asks from the passenger side of the car.

Ada takes a left as she navigates them through the city. "I told you. I need time to think."

"What's there to think about?" Eric asks, repeating the same question he has since he filled her in on the conversation with Tristan and the others. "These guys have the answers we've been looking for."

That they're aliens.

That they're Zodiac Guardians.

That they have a family with others like them.

The first part Ada could believe. She already suspected she wasn't from this world. But after that, the story gets harder and harder to believe. It progressively moves into fairytale territory.

Thirteen of them? All fighting a great evil like some supernatural Brady Bunch? That stuff doesn't happen to two social outcasts living on the streets. Plus, what she has with Eric is far too important to throw away on a promise from someone they just met.

"I want leverage, first." An upper hand.

Eric frowns. "What does that mean?"

Ada takes another turn and pulls into a parking lot. A large multi-story building is on the other side, Quentin Enterprises stamped across the front.

"I'm going to get the key first."

The moment she says it, Ada jumps out of the car, knowing Eric isn't going to like the idea. He exits more slowly, a thoughtful expression on his face. "And the key is here?" he indicates toward the shiny, glass-fronted offices.

"Yep," Ada says cheerfully. "I tracked the Solomon guy down. He had an office and apartment on the west end, but recently moved out without a trace. I may or may not have done a little hacking and found his IP address." She glances at the building. "And that IP address is now here."

"As in, right now?"

"Yep. That's where the key is."

Eric spears his fingers into his hair, a surefire sign he's more agitated than he's letting on. "I don't think this is a good idea."

Ada crosses her arms. "What if this whole thing is a twisted scheme to get the key? What if they're FBI, Eric?"

If she's caught, she loses everything. And by everything, that means Eric. The sweet guy standing across from her *is* her whole world.

He frowns. "They're not. I can tell."

"Sometimes, just because we want something to be true, doesn't mean it is," she says softly.

"And what if they're telling the truth, Ada?" he asks stubbornly. "What if we've finally got the answers we're looking for?"

Eric doesn't say it, but Ada hears the question that would be echoing through his head.

What if they've found their family?

She clutches the locket at her throat, conscious it's a defensive movement, but unable to stop herself. She wants that as much as Eric, but too much is riding on this.

If the FBI knows exactly what sort of carrot to dangle in front of them—family, belonging, answers—then this is most definitely a trap.

She has to be sure.

Ada sidles up to him. "If we can find the key, we can decode the message," she murmurs. "And when we meet, we bring it to them. If they're still talking family reunion after that, we know they're telling the truth."

Eric reaches out and she slips into his arms, relishing the sensations of their bodies fitting together.

He drops his forehead to hers. "Okay."

She draws in a sharp breath. She hadn't expected him to give in so easily. "You mean, we'll do it my way?"

"Yeah, we'll do it your way."

Ada notices the heaviness in his tone, and it tugs at something in her chest. Is he agreeing? Or just conceding defeat? Because the latter means they're no longer making decisions together. But before she can ask, Eric speaks again.

"But this time, I'm coming with you. Especially after what happened at the FBI offices."

Shoving away her unease, Ada smiles. "I was hoping you'd say that."

Not wanting to worry him, she hasn't mentioned that using her powers in such a big way drained her. For hours afterward she felt like a limp fish. If she hadn't woken up the next day feeling better, she would've been concerned.

If Eric's with her, there's less likelihood of needing to zap an entire roomful of people. She's not sure she wants to know what that would do to her energy levels. What if she collapsed there and then?

Eric glances at Quentin Enterprises. "So, what's the plan? It's too late to hack your way in."

"Maybe if we had time to order janitor uniforms, for me to print out some more fake passes, and we studied the security roster."

"Which we don't."

Not if they're meeting Tristan and the others tomorrow.

"Nope, we don't." Ada takes Eric's hand and tugs him toward the building. "That's why we're going to walk straight in."

He pulls back for a second, then falls into step beside her. "That's your plan?"

She keeps walking toward the entrance, throwing Eric a wink. "There are a couple more steps after that."

His brow contracts down, reminding her that he's not entirely comfortable with what they're doing. Ada shoves away her misgivings. When they have the key as a bargaining tool with Tristan and the others, Eric will see this was worth it.

She winces internally. Especially when he discovers what she has planned.

The sliding doors silently open, revealing a shiny, modern foyer. Ada notes the gray tiled floor. Of course it had to be tiled. Not a scrap of carpet to be seen.

There's a high counter to their left, an older, perfectly manicured male standing on the other side. "Welcome to Quentin Enterprises," he says warmly. "How can I help you?"

Ada smiles sweetly. "I'm here to see Mr. Davenport." A quick bit of research revealed he's one of the execs. An exec who has a teenage daughter, Courtney.

The receptionist—Niles according to his name tag—smiles politely. "Does he know you're here to see him?"

Ada flicks her hair. "The thing is, I totally left my phone at their place last night. It's all Courtney's fault. She

ADA 133

distracted me with photos of Zac Efron—" she widens her eyes—"don't you think he's only getting hotter the older he gets? Anyway, we lost track of time. I had to rush home, because my mom was totally going to ground me if I was late again."

Niles manages to maintain his smile throughout the story. "So, he's expecting you?"

Ada indicates with her head toward Eric. "I was supposed to be here earlier this morning, but I only just convinced my boyfriend to drive me over after I missed the bus. It took me, like, ages."

Eric crosses his arms. "Only because I'm not sure this is such a good idea."

Niles glances between the two of them. "I'll call—"

Ada's arm shoots forward. "But he might not let me go up there because I'm late," she says in a horrified tone. "We're talking about my cell phone here."

She practically hisses the final words, her eyes widening at the prospect of not being able to reunite with her non-existent technology.

Niles's eyebrows twitch, as if they were about to shoot up but he stops them. "I'm sure he'll understand."

"No, you can't," Ada wails. "If he says no, I won't get it back for, like, ever!"

Niles reaches for the phone, trying to look reassuring. "I'll explain the importance of your...phone."

Ada huffs, folding her arms on the marble counter. Eric slides her a 'this is your plan?' look. She almost rolls her eyes. Of course, this isn't her plan.

Unfortunately for her, it's going to involve a whole lot more pain.

Niles has just picked up the handset when Ada lets out a wail. She throws her head up and then straight down, onto the shiny, gray countertop. Just like she expected it would, her forehead slams into the unforgiving surface, bouncing straight back up like a bowling ball.

Just like she expected it would, it hurts like hell.

Following her momentum, Ada's head snaps back and she reels dramatically, then crumples to the floor.

"Ada!" Eric calls out in alarm.

He's instantly kneeling over her, and she realizes there's blood trickling from her nose. It seems she hit herself a little harder than she intended.

"Eric," she says quietly, her request embedded in that one word.

He works his magic even before she's finished uttering his name. The pain cracking her skull instantly washes away, leaving behind blessed nothingness, exactly like she knew he would.

"Oh Lord, oh Lord, oh Lord," Niles says over and over and he rushes around. He kneels down beside them. "Are you okay?"

Ada lifts her hand to her nose, gut clenching at the stickiness that coats her fingers. Still, although blood is trickling down her face, the pain is gone. She moans. "Am I dying?"

Eric slips an arm around her. "Can you stand?"

She makes a show of leaning heavily on him as Eric helps her to her feet. She pretends that her legs give out as she clings to him.

"Here," Niles says in alarm. "Come and sit in my office."

Ada glances at Eric in triumph as Niles leads them around the counter. But Eric's frowning so deeply that she's not sure the expression will be going away anytime soon. She didn't mean to spring a leak...

Behind the front desk, Niles leads them past the phone. Ada takes that moment to stumble again, giving the phone a surreptitious zap.

"Oh Lord," Niles moans as he quickly helps Eric scoop her up.

He uses his pass to open the door, ushering them into a small office and helping Ada into a chair. He yanks multiple tissues out of a box and passes the wad to her.

She takes them, making a point of trembling her hand. The moment he's close enough, she lurches forward to grasp his shoulder, stumbling a little. "Thank you," she says tearfully. "You probably just saved my life!"

Niles steps away the moment she releases him, his face looking like receptionist training never prepared him for something like this. Ada presses the tissues to her face, noting that the bleeding seems to have stopped as she collapses back into the chair.

He backs to the door. "I'll call...someone. They'll be able to help."

The moment he's gone, Ada leaps to her feet, holding up the pass she unclipped from his lanyard. "Mission accomplished."

Except even Eric's lips are downturned now. "I don't think all that was really necessary," he says, glancing at her tissue-covered nose.

Ada glances at the wad, noting that the bleeding has most definitely stopped. "I hadn't banked on the blood nose." She knew Eric would alleviate any pain banging her head. Although springing a leak added quite the dramatic flair. "And I knew you'd look after my headache."

"Ada..."

"Oh Lord, oh Lord, oh Lord," Niles moans from the front counter. Ada quickly sits back down, her hand pressing the tissues against her face. "Why does the phone stop working now?" He appears in the doorway, his face looking harried before turning away. "I'm going to go get someone," he calls over his shoulder, disappearing as he rushes to the back of the foyer.

With a quick wipe, Ada throws the tissues in a nearby trash can. "Shall we?"

She grasps Eric's hand before he can respond. He'll see that this was all worth it. If the Zodiacs—as they call themselves—are telling the truth, they need to know for sure. And the key will allow them to do that.

Eric will probably thank her for going to such lengths to protect them.

They slip out of the office, seeing the front desk is empty. Ada leads them to the elevators and uses Niles's pass to take them to the seventh floor. Even if someone goes looking for them, they'll assume they've gone to poor old Mr. Davenport's office, which is two floors up.

The elevator rises swiftly and silently, and Ada's heart rate picks up. She releases Eric's hand, hoping he won't notice her sweaty palms.

"Solomon's office is the first door on the right," she tells him. She draws in a steadying breath. "And I can't guarantee he's not there."

"What?" Eric demands incredulously. "You didn't tell me—"

The elevator *dings* softly, telling them they've arrived. Ada quickly steps out. "We've come too far now."

"Dammit, Ada." He strides past her. "You're not going in first."

Ada's heart leaps as he grabs the doorknob. She hadn't meant for him to put himself in danger like this. But before she can say anything, Eric pushes it open.

A gray-haired man leaps to his feet behind a desk. "What is the meaning of—"

His words are cut off as his eyes bulge and his hands grip his head as Eric stares at him. Solomon lets out a moan as he stumbles, one hand fumbling for his top drawer.

Ada instantly releases a bolt of electricity, making the man's body jerk backward. She ignores the jolt of lightheadedness as he hits the wall and slides down, unconscious.

"See?" Ada says chirpily. "Easy."

She quickly moves to the laptop on the desk while Eric hovers near Solomon. "Just be quick."

Glad to see the screen is open on a document—no need to try and get the password—she realizes what she's looking at.

"It's the key," she breathes.

Lines and lines of code fill the page, a cryptic waterfall of letters and numbers.

"No wonder they couldn't break it," she says. "These algorithms are fascinating!"

Eric shifts from foot to foot, obviously wanting to get out of here. "Can you crack it?"

"Of course I can," Ada scoffs. "I have Esther."

For a moment, she's tempted to take Solomon's computer, but she quickly changes her mind. It could have a tracer on it of some sort. She slips in a thumb drive and easily downloads everything she needs then deletes it. She holds it up to show Eric. "Got it."

For the first time, his face almost relaxes. "Good. Let's get going."

They've just made it to the door when a groan sounds from behind them. They spin around, but Solomon is still collapsed against the wall.

"Your locket..." he mutters. "I can tell you about it."

Ada wraps her hand around it. Her only link to her family, she's never been able to open it. No matter how hard she hit it, zapped it, or tried to pry it apart with any tool she could find.

How would this guy know anything about it?

She hesitates, then frowns as she takes Eric's hand and walks out. This guy could be working with the Zodiacs for all she knows.

She has the key. It's only a matter of time before she decodes the message.

That's all she needs for now.

22

TRISTAN

I s there a better way to celebrate finding two Zodiac Guardians in one day than a fro-yo for breakfast? Tristan doesn't think so.

He practically skips through the door, already antici-pating the sweet, cold gummy bears getting stuck in his teeth. Hopefully Madge will give him the extra scoop like she usually does.

The inside of the café is empty, but Tristan expected it to be. He couldn't get Jareth and Veronica out of bed to come with him, no matter how much he sang *Oh What a Beautiful Morning* in their doorway. At the top of his lungs. As he fired a party popper.

Tristan checks his phone as he heads to the counter, making sure he hasn't missed anything from Eric. He feels certain that he'll contact him sometime today. The look in his eyes—the realization that he's not alone—had told Tristan everything. This guy was looking for somewhere to belong, and he was excited that he might have finally found it.

There was just Dyad—Ada—to convince.

Surely that shouldn't take long? Surely Ada will see what Eric has—that they belong with the Zodiacs.

"Stop it," says a laughing voice.

A laughing voice Tristan recognizes.

He stalls a few feet shy of the counter, surprised. "Brielle?"

She looks up, startled, the smile that had lit up her face dropping like its strings were just cut. "Tristan. What are you doing here?"

"Getting a celebratory breakfast fro-yo," he says, not liking the same plunging sensation in his gut. His gaze slips past Brielle to the person she was talking to, and it sure as pitch isn't Madge.

A guy with dark hair and piercing eyes is standing next to Brielle. Closer than Tristan would've expected. The guy grins, jamming his hands in his pockets. He has bad boy written all over him.

Instantly, Tristan isn't sure he likes him.

Brielle quickly steps to the counter. "Did you want your usual?"

Tristan drags his gaze away from her coworker. "I didn't know you got a job at Creamy Dreams." He tries not to make the question accusatory, as if this is something *friends* would share with each other, but he's not entirely sure he succeeds.

A delicate pink flames over her cheeks. "I only applied the other day and today is my first shift."

The guy saunters forward. "Mine, too." He glances at Brielle. "It's our first time," he murmurs.

Something hot and searing scorches through Tristan's veins. The guy is openly flirting with Brielle!

"Stop it," she hisses, humor along with embarrassment evident in her voice. "Kerrim, this is Tristan, a good friend of mine. Tristan, this is Kerrim. It's also his first shift here."

Tristan grits his teeth as Kerrim holds his hand out to shake. Tristan grasps it, noting the strong confident grip. He makes sure he squeezes just enough to let Kerrim know that he's more than capable of holding his own. That he'll protect Brielle from guys like him with everything he has.

After a hard, sharp shake, they release. Kerrim's eyes glint with something Tristan can't name. He's liking him less and less by the minute.

Brielle clears her throat. "Why don't you sit down and I'll bring you your usual, Tristan?"

Tristan considers turning around and leaving, but he dismisses the idea before it's barely born. He's here to celebrate, and that's what he's going to do, dammit.

Slipping onto the seat at their usual table, Tristan checks his phone again. The screen is still blank. Eric probably isn't even up yet.

Unlike Brielle.

And Kerrim.

There's a giggle from behind the counter and Tristan's shoulders stiffen as the same scorching emotion flares through him again. His hand tightens around his cell phone as he realizes what it is.

He's jealous.

Even though he has no right to be.

Brielle and he aren't an item. She doesn't want that between them anymore. No matter how much he wishes it were otherwise.

Which means Brielle can flirt, date, hook up with whomever the pitch she wants. Tristan has to consciously release his phone before he shatters it. His mind might know that, but his heart is having the equivalent of a toddler tantrum. It refuses to consider that's an option.

He and Brielle—

He shakes his head. He and Brielle can never be. And if she can find love, while Tristan's duty is to find his soulmate —then that's a good thing.

"Here you go," Brielle says softly, sliding his fro-yo in front of him. It's a mountain of gummy bears, just like when Madge makes it.

And yet, Tristan has never felt less like a fro-yo .

He grips it and pulls it closer. "Thanks."

To his surprise, Brielle sits down across from him. "Two, huh?"

Two Zodiac Guardians. "Yeah," he says, poking one of the jelly bears down into the creamy dessert. Deep down, like it's drowning under the weight of the world it was happily sitting on top of a moment ago. "It's pretty exciting."

"It really is," she says. She fiddles with her nails. "Have you heard from Eric?"

Tristan shakes his head. "Hopefully soon." Silence descends between them again and Tristan inwardly frowns. They'd only just got back to friends status and now this.

"So, you've got a job."

Brielle nods. "With Frank in jail, I wanted to make sure I could help out wherever I can."

Always thinking of others. Always making sure she's not a burden. Tristan leans forward a little. Brielle only sees the good in people. "Just be careful with him, okay?" He indicates with his head toward the counter.

She frowns. "I can take care of myself."

"I know. You're a kick ass Zodiac. But there's something about him…"

Brielle's lips press together as she stares at him. Tristan's gaze drops to his fro-yo. He's acting like a jealous ex-boyfriend.

And although that's a pretty accurate description, he's also looking out for her as a friend. As a fellow Zodiac. "I just don't want to see you get hurt."

Brielle draws back, increasing the distance between them.

"Why don't you talk to your soulmate about it?" she asks quietly.

Tristan stills, the words feeling like a slap. The moment Ada appeared, his Gemini twin no longer became a nebulous barrier between them. His soulmate became a very real possibility. He clenches his fists. "We don't know which Zodiac Ada is," he points out.

"But she could be the other Gemini," Brielle replies instantly.

There's nothing Tristan can say. She's right. Ada could be his soulmate. And if she is, the battle against Chardis just tipped in their favor in a big way.

Brielle sighs. "I just want you to be happy, Tristan."

He holds her gaze for long seconds, seeing the honesty in her moss green eyes, along with the sadness that echoes in his soul. For a brief second, he wonders if it's the same for Brielle.

That he wants the same for her. But despite all that, it doesn't stop the way he feels about her.

"Bri, can you show me how to use this dispenser again?" Kerrim calls out.

Tristan grinds his teeth together. *Bri?*

She pushes to her feet, shaking her head. "Madge showed me just like she showed you."

Kerrim grins, his gaze nowhere but Brielle. "But you explain it so much better."

Tristan shoots to his feet. "I'm going to head out. I'll let you know if I hear anything."

Brielle pauses on her way back to the counter. "You're leaving your fro-yo?"

But he's already got his hand on the door. "Ah, no. It's probably not the best thing to have for breakfast." He pats his stomach. "You know me, health freak and all that."

In fact, he's not sure he'll want a fro-yo ever again.

He's out the door before Brielle can respond. Outside, he sets up a determined stride back home. He'll head straight to the gym and do a work out. Possibly for the rest of the day.

His phone dings as he reaches the end of the block. A glance at the screen reveals Eric's name.

Ada agreed to meet. At the cemetery. Tomorrow, two o'clock.

Tristan's lips twitch. She's chosen somewhere public, but quiet. Clever.

He quickly types a response. *"We'll be there. Looking forward to talking."*

And bringing them all together.

Eight Zodiacs. Two in one day. For Zarius, that's the equivalent of winning the lotto.

And yet the spring in Tristan's step doesn't return. In fact, he jams his hands in his pockets and hunches his shoulders, his feet trudging over the pavement.

Tomorrow they'll be two stronger.

Tomorrow, he'll find out if Ada is his soulmate.

23

BRIELLE

"So, I'll pick you up tonight around seven?" Kerrim asks as they walk out the door of Creamy Dreams after a successful first shift.

Brielle glances at him with surprise, and he waggles his thick eyebrows playfully.

"I wasn't aware we'd made concrete plans," she says, her voice wavering with uncertainty.

"Exactly, so I'm making them now." His charm is radiant, and it's definitely having an effect on her.

She giggles nervously, looking down at her feet. "I'm not so sure tonight will work. I have a second job to go to now, and I have no idea when I'll get out." She's expected at Richard Sinclair's office in twenty minutes, and while it's true that she doesn't know how long this task will take, she's also not entirely sure she's ready to go on a date with Kerrim yet.

Working with him today was the most fun she's had in a long time, and she doesn't completely hate the uncomfortable tingle that fills her insides whenever she's around him. But she has so many other things to focus on right now—the internship and getting the key so they can decode the message, trying to get Frank out of jail, getting the two newest Zodiacs to join their team.

Finding out if Ada really is the Gemini Twin…

Kerrim nods, but his sexy grin doesn't look the least bit discouraged. "All work and no play makes Brielle a dull girl. Although I highly doubt there's anything dull about you." He winks, and her insides tighten and melt at the same time. "Text me when you're done, and I promise I'll make it worth your while."

Pretty sure her entire body has flamed a bright pink, she stammers, "Okay," and walks away before she can do something truly embarrassing.

No sooner does she turn in the other direction than her phone rings in her jeans pocket. She pulls it out, hoping it might be Bea with news.

Instead, it's Mr. Sinclair.

Her jaw muscles clenching instinctively, she puts the phone to her ear. "Hello?"

"Hello Brielle, there's been a change of plan." His voice holds a strange note to it, but she can't decipher what it is. It almost sounds tinny, guarded. "Due to unforeseen complications, I will not be able to meet you this afternoon. Instead, I would like you to meet with an associate. I have texted you the address."

"Oh…okay," she says, suspicion coiling up her spine. "Wh—"

"He's expecting you in fifteen minutes," Mr. Sinclair cuts her off. "Don't be late." And then he hangs up.

That was by far the weirdest phone call she's ever received. Something about this doesn't sound right, but what other choice does she have if she wants to use Mr. Sinclair to clear Frank's name?

She opens the text and looks at the address. It's not too

far away. She can easily ride her bike there. Figuring she'd be wise to let someone know where she's going, she sends Cassandra a quick text, then swings her leg over her bike and heads down the road.

Before she can get out of the Creamy Dreams parking lot, a shiny, gorgeous black Mustang with two red racing stripes over the top pulls in front of her, blocking her path.

She makes a warning frown at the darkened windows, and to her surprise, the front passenger window rolls down.

"Need a lift?" Kerrim asks.

Her eyes widen. "*This* is your car?"

He shrugs. "It gets me where I need to go. It can do the same for you."

His charm is like a siren call, beckoning her to lower her defenses and follow it.

She swallows and shakes her head. "It's okay, I've got my bike."

He tilts in his head in a come hither gesture. "Come on. Wherever you're going, I can get you there a lot faster than that rust bucket can. No offense." Another wink, and her legs suddenly feel like noodles.

It would be nice not to have to ride. What's the harm?

Sighing, she hops off her bike, and Kerrim comes around to pick it up and fasten it to the top rack of his racy sports car. Then he opens the passenger door for her.

"Mi-lady," he says like an old fashioned gentleman as he waits for her to get in.

Hiding her blush with her hair, she slides in and buckles her seat belt. He gets into the driver's seat and punches the stick into gear.

"Where to?"

She shows him the address on her phone and he takes it from her, turning on navigation.

"So, what's your second job?" he asks as they zoom onto the road.

"I'm interning for an accounting firm," she says.

Kerrim frowns and glances at the address on the phone. "And it's *there?*"

"I've been instructed to meet someone there," she answers vaguely.

"Sounds kinda shady to me." He pops the clutch into third and the powerful vehicle roars like it really does have four hundred horses under its hood.

She doesn't say anything, only because it sounds kinda shady to her, too. What could Mr. Sinclair have up his sleeve?

Kerrim accepts her silence as answer enough. "So, that guy who came in today. Tristan. Did I sense some tension there?"

Her heart trips at the sound of Kerrim saying Tristan's name. She swallows. "Uh, yeah. We kinda, sorta dated. Very briefly. But he's still my best friend."

Kerrim nods, keeping his eyes trained on the road. "Sounds like he might not have gotten the memo that it's over between you two."

She looks down at her lap, then out her window. "It would never have worked. He's hung up on someone else."

Kerrim's fingers tap against the steering wheel. "And...are you hung up on him?"

Brielle bites her lip and turns to him. Even if she could, she doesn't want to lie to her prospective new guy. "Kinda."

He smirks, the corner of his lips curling in a devilish way that makes her heart race. "Maybe I can help you forget about him."

She doesn't say anything, but she's sure the beet red that's now coloring her face says everything for her.

Maybe you can...

They pull into a yard loaded with stacked shipping containers as far as the eye can see.

Brielle leans forward and looks around skeptically. "Are you sure we're in the right place?"

"No, but Siri is," Kerrim says, tapping the screen of her phone that's displaying a happy face that says they've reached their destination. He slides the stick into park. "Are you sure you don't want me to wait with you?"

Brielle sits in the seat like a lead weight, debating whether or not to take him up on his offer. Then she remembers she's a Zodiac Guardian, and he's only human. If something sketchy is about to go down, she wants him as far away from it as possible.

She reaches for the handle. "No, I'll be fine. I'll text you tonight when I'm finished." When his dubious frown doesn't budge, she smiles reassuringly. "You might be surprised that I don't need anyone to rescue me. That I can take care of myself."

His wry smirk returns. "Of that, I have no doubt." He leans across her and pulls on her handle, opening her door for her. "Good luck. I'll be waiting for that text."

"Thanks, Kerrim. I really appreciate this." She pulls herself out of the low riding car, takes her bike off the rack, then hovers by the door before closing it. "Your name. I've been curious. Where does it come from?"

"Let me take you out and I might tell you." His impishly curling lips are the last thing she sees before he pulls the passenger door closed, then slowly drives away.

Oh boy, I'm in trouble, she tells herself as she urges the butterflies in her stomach to cease their fluttering. She's got bigger fish to fry.

She turns to the shipping yard, eyes diligently scanning for signs of movement. Why the pitch would Mr. Sinclair have her meet anyone here?

Standing there in an echoing quiet for the longest time, she kicks a rock into the open space to test for movement. Nothing happens.

"Hello?" she calls out. Nothing but the subtle woosh of distant waves beyond the yard responds to her.

Maybe Mr. Sinclair gave her the wrong address. He must have. There's no way she could be meant to meet anyone professional here.

She pulls out her phone to text Kerrim to come back.

"Good afternoon, Miss Pierce," says that familiar southern drawl.

Brielle looks up to see Solomon stepping out from behind a rusting yellow container. His usually slicked back salt-and-pepper hair is slightly disheveled, but his suit still looks clean.

This is the person Mr. Sinclair wanted her to meet? Pitch, she should have known this was a trap!

"Mr. Gray," she says, straightening her posture to at least look unafraid. "What are we doing here?"

"Well darlin', what say we skip all the baloney and lay all our cards on the table," he says, clasping his hands at his waist and stepping closer. "I know that you're a Zodiac Guardian, and you know that I'm, well, let's just say, on the winning team."

She says nothing, but braces herself, the word *Akash* on the tip of her tongue to use at a moment's notice. She also steals a quick glance in either direction for signs of Skins. There's no wind today, so if something moves when it shouldn't, she'll know.

"Someone attacked me at my new apartment yesterday, and I believe it was one of your little friends," he continues, sauntering in the beginning of a wide circle with his southern swagger. "They stole something from me."

Brielle has no idea what he's talking about. They've been

looking for Solomon, and she's sure none of them found him, or they would have told her.

"I don't know who attacked you, but I assure you—"

"Now Miss Pierce, I thought we were going to be honest with each other," he cuts her off.

She grits her teeth. "If you know as much as you claim to, then you know that I *can't* lie. If I say something, it must be the truth. And I'm telling you I have no idea who attacked you. What did they steal that was so important?" Did they take the box from him? The one he ran away with? If so, she must find out who they are so she can retrieve it.

"As a matter of fact, they stole the very thing that was going to be handed to you by our joint benefactor," he replies, still calm as a warm summer day. "Which makes us certain you knew of its true value."

Her eyes betray her and widen. "The key," the word escapes her mouth.

"So you do know. I knew you were a clever girl."

"If we had the key, you and I wouldn't be having this conversation," she promises. "We would be using it."

He regards her with narrowed eyes. Then nods. "I suspected as much, but we had to be sure. That means, for this one moment only, the Zodiacs and I are in need of the same thing. Perhaps we can work together."

She wants to declare that there's no way in pitch that the Zodiacs will help him, or Mr. Sinclair, but she has to be wary. "What do you want from me, Solomon? Why did Richard Sinclair hire you to help me? If you knew I was a Zodiac, and you're clearly working for Chardis, why not let me go to jail and get rid of one of your enemies?"

Solomon smirks and nods. "That is where you're mistaken, Miss Pierce. We are not Chardis's minions. We chose to assist him to benefit ourselves. We are not—now what is it you call them—Skins? We are"—he tilts his head back and forth—"employees, you could say. And as such, we had to look out for a better interest. We had reason to believe you could be the missing Gemini Princess. If such a thing were true, we might have to reconsider our allegiances. Like I said before, we want to be on the winning side. And having the Geminis united would put the Zodiacs on the winning side."

They thought she could be the other Gemini. That's why they've been helping her. She's truly sorry to disappoint them.

"Well, I'm not," she says, struggling to keep her shoulders from sagging with the defeat that has weighed so heavily on her since she found out she wasn't. "But, we may have found her."

Solomon processes that for a moment. "The couple who attacked me, the girl radiated power. Is she whom you're referring to?"

"What did they look like?" Brielle is truly eager for the answer.

"The girl had a mess of orange curls, and the guy was stoic with blond hair. Somehow, they used some unseen force to cripple me with pain."

Eric. The guy was undoubtedly Eric. She'll never forget the way Tristan had crumpled under Eric's pain power.

Brielle's lack of response seems to answer Solomon's question.

"So you *think* you found her, but you're not certain?"

Brielle looks away. "She hasn't come to us to touch the stones."

"I see," Solomon says, and Brielle realizes she's made a grave mistake. She needs Solomon to believe that they really have found the missing Gemini, that they have a hand over Chardis. They don't need more enemies. "Well now, just what are we going to do about this?"

Before Brielle can even blink edgewise, a handful of large black SUVs pull into the parking lot, and dozens of FBI agents in bulletproof vests storm out with guns raised.

Solomon shoots her an accusing glare, but the utter astonishment that must be clear on her face dissolves it as the feds surround and detain him.

Several of them tow him roughly toward one of the SUVs as the rest scan the perimeter for hiding accomplices, only to find what she already knew—he's alone. They struggle to shove him to the backseat, and he shouts out to her, "The key's in Dyad's necklace!"

As Jack Cadbury emerges from the horde toward her, she's certain of two things:

One, she's potentially in a lot of trouble just for being here.

And two, her internship with Mr. Sinclair, and only hope at clearing her father's name, is over.

JACK

14:30

"Hello, Brielle."

She crosses her arms, lifting her chin. "Agent Cadbury."

As two of the SUVs roar away, taking the bastard Solomon with them, Jack pins Brielle with a glare. Of course she was here, meeting with the slimy lawyer. Solomon is the one who swooped in and had Brielle released when Jack was questioning her. If she, Tristan and the others hadn't saved Logan's life...

"What are you doing here?" he asks quietly.

Her chin lifts another notch. "Are you going to arrest me?"

Jack's mind works in overdrive, trying to think of a reason he could haul her in. She was close to cracking last time, he could feel it. "That depends. What are you doing here, Miss Pierce?"

"I was running an errand. I had no idea Solomon would be here."

Jack studies Brielle carefully. She said the words simply, holding his gaze. She's either telling the truth, or she's a damned good liar. According to Logan and Veronica, she's telling the truth. "What did Solomon want?"

"Something had been stolen from him. A key."

Jack stills. The key the FBI has been trying to decipher for weeks now. "And Dyad has it?" he asks, remembering Solomon's shouted words as he was being arrested.

Brielle shrugs. "Apparently."

Jack's mind works quickly. Dyad has been on the FBI's most wanted list for years. He even tried to catch the slippery hacker himself, years ago. But with everything that's going on, he didn't make the link that Dyad was probably involved in all this. Dammit.

Brielle's arms tighten and Jack recognizes the gesture for what it is—a nervous one. He angles his head. "Who is this Dyad? Do you know him?"

The girl's eyes widen imperceptibly, but then her face hardens. "Are you arresting me, Agent Cadbury?"

Jack's muscles tighten. He has Solomon to question, which is what he has to focus on. And there's a truce with these…Zodiacs.

"Not today," he grinds out.

But that doesn't mean he won't be hauling her in at a later date. Whatever agreement they have is gone the moment Jack has some solid evidence. Especially if Solomon gives him something he can use to pin Tristan and his friends. All Jack needs is a shred of evidence that they're part of the evil that's slowly spreading through this city and he's going to do everything he can to make sure they'll be locked away for life.

Brielle hurries past him, grabs the bike that wasn't far away, and pedals away.

One of his operatives steps closer. "Sir?"

Jack nods curtly. "We have an interrogation to undertake."

Spinning on his heel, he climbs into the remaining SUV. The vehicle roars away, passing Brielle on the way. She keeps her head down, never glancing up.

Jack settles into his seat, jaw working. She and the others can wait. He presses the speed dial on his cell phone, dialing Logan.

First, he's going to do whatever it takes to get Solomon to talk.

Then, Dyad's going on Nebula's most wanted list.

24

CASSANDRA

"I'm so sorry about everything you've been through." Cassandra squeezes tighter as she cuddles Logan in his car outside of the diner.

They've been stealing as many moments like this as they can since his release from the hospital. Jack Cadbury believes Logan is just dating Cassandra to gain intel, so they've been keeping their interludes out of his sight as much as possible. She knows the secrecy is a strain on Logan, but she can't handle not seeing him, especially after he was held and beaten by the very same company his father works for, only days after being let go from the hospital with a gunshot wound in remission.

He presses her against him in a gesture meant to soothe. "I've prepared myself for this lifestyle my entire life. And those nanites are pretty damn impressive." He raises a wry brow "I just never realized the job I was destined for was protecting the entire Universe, and not just the United States."

"Still," she says, chewing on her bottom lip. "It should have been me to go with you to the FBI instead of Jareth."

"If you had, we would have both been caught that much sooner," he says on a sigh. "At least Jareth has the ability to disguise his face. Otherwise he would have been in the same shipwrecked boat as me."

"Maybe, but I can protect you better than he can." She holds up her hand and lets it glow in the dim light of the car.

He chuckles. "Yes. My knight in shining armor. Knightess? What's the female term for knight?"

She cocks her head up at him, giving him a catty frown. "Um, as Brienne of Tarth would tell you, Knights can be men or women, thank you very much."

He laughs hard and slaps his knee at her Games of Thrones reference. "So, does that make me Jaime Lannister?"

Her lips twist in a disgusted grimace. "Please. The last thing I want to do right now is imagine you with your sister. I mean, I guess technically, you two aren't actually related, but—"

"Okay, reel back that overactive imagination of yours," he says, holding her closer. "And besides, you're way too beautiful to be Brienne of Tarth. You're more like Daenerys Targaryen. With all the fire to boot."

"So, then, you're Jon Snow?" She turns a smartass smile on him. "What is with you and incest analogies today?"

He shakes his head in mild frustration. "You know what, let's get away from Game of Thrones. You started it, but I'm ending it."

She laughs, savoring the freedom of this brief escape. "Okay, fine. But if you start comparing us to Luke and Leia, I'm out."

His frown deepens, and she laughs even harder.

Her glee is broken by the blast of Demi Lovato's Confident from her pocket. She pulls out her phone.

And her eyes widen as her entire body tenses.

"Who is it?" Logan asks, clearly seeing the shock she's frozen into.

"It's my...dad." She croaks out the last word.

"Oh, good. I've got a few choice words for him." He reaches for the phone.

She instinctively pulls it away. "No. He's my problem to deal with." She lets out a long breath, then answers. "Hello, daddy dearest," she says in her most obnoxiously cheerful voice.

"Where's Solomon?" His voice is laced with more steel than she's ever heard before, and she fights the urge to cringe, remembering that he's not here to hit her, and that she wouldn't take it anyway.

"What are you talking about?" The mention of Solomon's name has her interest blazing. Why would he think she knows? She and Brielle have been trying to find him for days.

"I tasked your little friend with meeting him today, and he's been unreachable ever since," he responds, all business with an unmistakable hint of accusation.

Little friend? "Brielle?" she wonders aloud.

"Don't play dumb," he scolds. "You know exactly what I'm talking about. Now tell me what you've done with him."

The anger boils inside her so quickly that she can hardly contain it. She's done bowing to him in any way, shape or form. "Not only did I not have any idea Brielle was supposed to meet him, but I also have no clue where your little minion might have run off to. So why don't you take a good long look at yourself and get a better handle on your associates before you go pointing fingers at innocent little girls." She only realizes that she's practically shouting by the end of it because Logan is squinting beside her.

The other end is quiet for a moment, and she begins to wonder if he hung up on her. She checks her phone to see that the minutes are still counting the length of the call.

"I don't trust you—" he begins, then is interrupted by the unmistakable voice of his secretary telling him, "Sir, you've got an urgent call on line two." Without a word, he places Cassandra on hold, and she's forced to listen to the agonizing elevator music they have as their hold theme. She considers hanging up on him, but she's too invested to give up now.

After a few minutes of her tugging at the loose thread of a rip in her jeans and Logan comfortingly patting the top of her hand, her dad finally picks back up. "Apparently, there have been some complications."

Her dad says nothing else to clarify the situation, and she throws her hands up. "What the hell does that mean?"

He sighs. "We were prepared to offer a sort of...truce to the Zodiacs." He gives a dry chortle. "How fateful that my own daughter ended up to be one." He sighs lengthily. "At any rate, consider Brielle's laughable internship on hold until further notice. Would you be a dear and let her know for me?"

Cassandra opens her mouth to chew him out, but the line goes dead. And she's left sitting in the front passenger's seat with her mouth hanging open.

"What happened?" Logan asks, squeezing the hand he was just patting.

"I...don't really know. But shit just got real."

JACK

16:40

Jack glares at Solomon as he sits across from him inside the van, a Nebula agent on either side of him. "So, Dyad has the key."

Solomon lifts his chin, still managing to look haughty

despite his arms being cuffed behind him. "That's what I said." He smirks. "But I find the truth to be...malleable."

Jack curls his lip. "I bet you do."

"Haven't you already made up your mind anyway, Agent Cadbury?"

Jack leans forward, the determination to do whatever it takes to get info out of this slimy southern bastard vibrating through his body. "You can talk now, or you can talk in the interrogation room. It's up to you."

Solomon merely arches a contemptuous eyebrow, his lips tightly shut.

"Not everyone comes out of that room alive," Jack warns quietly.

Solomon smirks again. "You think I'm afraid to die?"

Jack's ulcer flares at those words. Those who have little to lose are the hardest to interrogate. It means the room will get...messy.

The van slows to a halt. "Roadworks," calls the driver from the front. "We'll take Fifth."

Jack pins Solomon with his gaze. "That'll give you more thinking time. People tend to underestimate how convincing pain can be."

But Solomon simply stares at the ceiling, feigning boredom. Jack leans back against the metal wall of the van, willing to play this game. In fact, it just means he's looking forward to wiping the expression off the smug bastard's face.

Suddenly, everyone jerks hard to the left as the van brakes. Jack's instantly on alert. "What's up?"

"Darned garbage truck just reversed straight out onto the road."

The detour, now this. Jack yanks out his firearm. "It's a decoy!"

But before Jack's words are out, there's a gunshot and the driver slumps over the wheel.

"Dammit!" he shouts. "Everyone get down!"

The passenger is shot dead before he can move. A volley of bullets pepper the side of the van, making Jack and the other agents instinctively duck. He grabs Solomon and pushes him to the floor as they all crouch low. They need to stay away from the windows.

Solomon grunts. "Send me outside and this is all over."

"Like hell I will," snaps Jack. Solomon has the answers he needs. About Dyad. About the box.

About the Zodiacs.

There's a flicker of movement beyond the windshield and it shatters as a bullet pierces it. The agent to Jack's left grunts as blood blooms across his temple. His body flattens as he splays on the floor, dead. Jack partially uncurls, sending out his own rapid-fire shots as the black-clad man leaps out of the way with inhuman speed.

"You can be alive or dead when I walk out of this van," says Solomon flatly. "It's up to you."

Jack glances at the remaining agent with him. He thinks of his children. Logan and Veronica would be orphans...

With a growl, he kicks Solomon, taking a small measure of satisfaction in the grunt it elicits as the man is propelled toward the back doors. They're shoved open by Solomon's momentum, and he tumbles onto the road.

A little part of Jack is hoping his trigger happy friends shoot him before they realize he's not Nebula.

But the air is devoid of deadly gunfire as Solomon rolls to a stop. He stands up, for once, his immaculate gray suit rumpled and twisted, then looks over his shoulder back at the van.

"It sure was lovely chatting," he drawls, disdain twisting his lips.

For a moment, Jack's tempted to shoot him there and then. But as much as he wants to see Solomon dead, so would be all the information he holds. And right now, that's far more valuable than his life.

It's just that Solomon knows it.

With an arrogant sneer, he saunters toward the garbage truck, somehow still looking superior despite the scuffed suit and handcuffs. Jack guarantees a getaway car will be just beyond it.

Jack waits, knowing these assholes could still finish them off. If that's the case, he'll go down taking as many as he can with him.

But silence reigns. Traffic has come to a standstill, a shootout that's only seen in movies having just played out on a New York street.

The agent across from him pulls out a small locket from his shirt and kisses it. "Daddy will be coming home today," he murmurs.

A moment later, the wail of sirens tells Jack that backup has arrived. Maybe he should've held out, but judging by the trembling hands on the agent across from him, he knows he made the right choice. Two families will remain intact today, unlike the three agents sprawled and still bleeding within the coffin he's now in.

That's three more lives that have been taken in the fight to keep Earth safe.

Three more the Zodiacs will be held responsible for.

25

TRISTAN

Tristan stares at the tombstones of his parents, the familiar grief dragging at his insides. At least the stabbing loss that could wrench away his ability to breathe for long seconds is gone. Now, it's just an aching throb that he knows will never go away.

"We're meeting two more today," he murmurs. "That will bring us to seven."

He tries to imagine Zarius and Tess's faces if they'd been alive to hear that news. Zarius would probably have needed to sit down. Tess wouldn't have been able to sit still.

They've come so far.

And yet, it feels like they're not getting any closer to defeating Chardis.

Tristan's shoulders feel like they've been compressed together and he can't figure out how to release them. The wormhole still exists and they don't have the key to decipher the message that arrived through it.

Something is coming. He can feel it.

He sighs, stretching his shoulders even though they feel

like they're about to snap. Ada and Eric will be here soon. That's two Zodiacs closer to winning.

To avenging his parents' deaths.

He swallows. And if Ada is the Gemini Twin then Chardis won't stand a chance...

There's a sound down the path and Tristan spins around. Brielle is rushing toward him, hair flying behind her. His heart lurches, as it always does, and he shoves away the feeling. Everything is way too complicated to go there right now. He steps forward. "Is everything okay?"

Brielle stops, panting a little. "Dyad stole the key from Solomon."

Frustration explodes through Tristan. "What?"

They need that key.

"And now Jack Cadbury has arrested Solomon."

Logan arrives, striding down the path, Cassandra by his side. "Dad just rang. Dyad has the key."

Tristan nods, bursts of simmering anger pounding his head. "Brielle just told me."

Logan glances at Brielle. "Dad said you met with him."

"Mr. Sinclair sent me to meet someone after saying there had been a change of plans—it must've been because the key was stolen. Solomon was waiting for me." She swallows, turning toward Cassandra. "He said he and Mr. Sinclair work for Chardis, but they're not Skins."

Cassandra gasps, then snaps her mouth closed. "That actually makes total sense."

Logan grasps her hand, intertwining their fingers in a silent show of support.

Tristan rubs his temples. "So Ada has the key."

Surely that's got to be a good thing.

"Except she's now on both the FBI's and Nebula's hit list," Logan says grimly.

"Great," Tristan mutters. Just freaking great.

Ada joining the Zodiacs is now more important than ever.

Jareth and Veronica hurry over from his parents' memorial, no doubt having noticed the intensity of the conversation. Logan quickly gets them up to speed.

Veronica's lips thin. "Dad didn't call me."

"He might yet," Jareth points out.

Veronica nods, but her gaze drops to her shoes. It obviously still stings that Jack doesn't quite trust her as much as Logan.

Could things be any more complicated?

"At least Ada and Eric will be here shortly," Brielle points out.

Tristan nods, grateful for the reminder that this could all be looking up very soon. If Ada joins them, she'll have the protection of the Zodiacs. And if she has the key, they can finally find out what the message is.

He withdraws the flat box he had tucked in his jacket, feeling exposed having it out in the open.

Brielle's eyes widen. "You brought the stones?"

He nods, his gaze holding hers. "It's the only way we'll know for sure."

Everyone falls silent and Tristan wonders if the others are aware of the significance of what's about to happen. Have they considered that Ada might be his soulmate, too?

Jareth clears his throat. "How many stones are in there?"

"Three," Tristan says quietly. "Some Zodiacs already have theirs. We have the diamond for Aries, lapis lazuli for Pisces, and...the other tanzanite."

The identical stone to his.

"So she could be any one of those," Cassandra points out.

Tristan nods, realizing his teammates are trying to be some sort of weird cheer squad. It's as if none of them want Ada to be the Gemini.

His gaze, his heart, ache to connect with Brielle, but he glances at his phone instead, checking the time. "They're late," he mutters.

The prospect that Ada and Eric might ghost them hits Tristan like a slap. What if they've made a run for it...

His cell dings and Eric's name appears on the screen, almost as if they knew Tristan was considering freaking the flip out.

"What is it?" Logan asks, his voice heavy with suspicion. It seems he's on edge as much as Tristan is.

"A text from Eric."

The others crowd in as Tristan opens it, his breath frozen in his lungs.

They've decided they're not coming.

They've fled the country.

Nebula has already captured them.

But none of those words appear on the screen. A collection of gasps ricochet around him from the other Zodiacs.

"She cracked the code," Tristan says in amazement.

And she sent it to them in a freaking text!

26

ADA

I t took Ada far longer to crack the key than she thought. She and Esther barely slept, barely ate, heck, she's not even sure they blinked last night.

It was clear early on that there were multiple encryptions, a cascade encoding the message multiple times. Solomon's key had hacked the first level and had reached a dead end. Which means there was more than one key.

With the first key already solved, Ada had set to work on the second one.

At about midnight, Eric had brought food and drink. Ada took an absent minded sip of the soda, but then completely forgot it existed. It's like she and Esther became one, numbers and letters being manipulated, reversed, and collated as they built algorithm on algorithm. Words like superencipherment, independent initialization, and asymmetric key had whirled around alongside them. Eric had reclined the driver's seat and made himself as comfortable as he could. It was his soft snores that became the comforting background as Ada continued to work.

She ciphered the second key not long later and watched

with amazement as the strange symbols that the message arrived in morphed into letters. A jumbled, incomprehensible mess of letters, but letters nonetheless.

Ada was now working with units of the alphabet from this planet. Progress!

When Eric woke up just as morning sunbeams touched the hood of the car, Ada had been waiting. Her eyes were gritty and her head felt wooly, but there was no way she could've slept.

Not after she cracked the code and the message was now printed on Esther's screen.

Eric had sat up quickly, a concerned frown on his face. "What is it?"

"I know what it says," she'd said quietly.

Eric's frown had deepened, probably because she was using the same tone of voice someone would use to convey the news of the death of a loved one. The hard knot of dread in her stomach feels like she just did.

"Show me," he'd said quietly.

Ada had turned Esther's screen around to face him.

Now, as she's just pressed the send button on Eric's phone, she waits for Tristan to receive the same message.

Destruction is coming my son.

It's ominous.

It's full of menace.

And Ada has no idea what it means.

Eric lets out a breath she hadn't realized he'd been holding. "So, we can go see them now?"

Ada nods resolutely. "They have what they wanted. Let's see what they say."

Will Tristan and the others turn out to be nothing but a decoy, or has everything they've been saying been true?

Have she and Eric finally found the answers as to why they're like this?

Eric smiles, and the way his face lights up robs Ada of breath. "Good. You're going to really connect with these guys. I just know it."

Ada rolls her eyes. "Unless they're FBI."

Although as she says the words, she realizes she's just going through the motions. She doesn't believe Tristan and the others are FBI, not deep down. There's no way she would've agreed to meet them if she thought they were.

They climb out of the car and fall in, side by side. Ada takes Eric's hand, tingles dancing along her skin, and he winces.

"Sorry," she murmurs.

She's more wound up about this meeting than she realized.

Eric grins. "I'm excited, too."

Ada shakes her hand out, as if ridding herself of the electrical charge that had built up. If Tristan is who he said he is, then he'll be able to explain why she has so little control over her powers.

She and Eric could be a real couple, in every sense of the world. They'd finally be together in the one way they've never been able to be. The thought has joy singing through her veins.

They enter the gates of the cemetery and take the path to the agreed meeting point. Tristan had seemed familiar with the place as he suggested a grassed area at the back.

They take a right, and Ada sees the group of teens standing beside some headstones. A sculpture of some brightly colored daisies isn't far away.

Ada's pulse trips over itself. This is getting real.

She sees Tristan standing in the center, the others fanned out on either side of him. A brunette hovers by his right, and Ada realizes there's something familiar about her. In fact, the girl's eyes widen with recognition.

But then there's movement on the girl's other side and Ada's gaze is drawn further along. The blonde bombshell that was with Tristan at the FBI offices has just subtly moved closer to the brunette. Ada's about to look away when she sees who's standing next to the blonde.

She gasps, stopping several feet away. Betrayal she has no right to feel slices through her. "It's a trap!"

Eric tenses beside her.

Tristan freezes. "What? No."

Ada points furiously at the guy standing beside the blonde. "You thought I wouldn't recognize him?" she demands angrily. "That's Jack Cadbury's son!"

Logan Cadbury's brows shoot up. He opens his mouth to speak, but Ada continues.

"Yes, I've done my research." She scans the others in the group, another jolt of recognition shredding at her chest. "And that's Veronica, his daughter."

Eric steps in closer to her. "Is that true?"

Tristan holds out his hands, his face looking panicked. "No, I mean, yes. They're Jack's children, but they're both with us."

"Of course they are," Ada explodes. Anger has electricity crackling up her spine. She doesn't remember ever being this furious. But then again, she was never stupid enough to let herself believe. "Because you're FBI!"

The blonde stiffens, flicking her glossy hair over her shoulder. "We've been over this. We're not FBI. In fact, we're probably just as high on Jack's wanted list as you are."

Ada takes a step back, then another. Bitterness stains her tongue, but she ignores it. She and Eric have just walked into a trap, lured by the promise of answers and belonging. If she has to zap every one of these liars and traitors to get away, then so be it.

Tristan must sense her intentions, because he presses his

palms forward as he shuffles his feet, trying to regain some of the distance between them. "It's a long and complicated story," he says quietly, sensing that Ada's on the edge of fight or flight. "But we can explain it all to you. Logan is a Zodiac, just like you are. Veronica knows everything because she's with Jareth, another Zodiac. They both have kept everything they know from Jack."

"You expect me to believe that?" Ada almost shouts. "How much of a fool do you take me for?"

Tristan shakes his head. "No one thinks you're a fool, Ada." His gaze flickers to his right. "Show her, Logan."

But before Logan can even blink, Ada throws out a bolt of energy. He tumbles backward, arms flying out wide as he lands on his backside. The blonde cries out as she kneels over him. When she sees that Logan's fine—all Ada did was use enough energy to knock him on his ass...and maybe give his ticker a buzz—the blonde raises furious golden eyes to Ada.

Tristan steps in front of her. "No, Cassandra. We won't fight her."

Cassandra mutters something unintelligible but doesn't move.

Ada holds her hands out in a similar fashion to the way Tristan just was, but while his was a conciliatory gesture, hers is a warning. Anyone comes any closer and she'll nuke them.

"We're leaving now," she says through gritted teeth. "You got your message, there's nothing else you need from us."

"Thank you for deciphering it," Tristan says quietly. "But you're far more important than what Chardis had to say."

That destruction is coming. And that he has a son, waiting here on Earth to receive the message.

Eric steps closer to Ada. "You said you could prove we're like you."

Ada stiffens, not liking that Eric's still talking as if they still want to hear what Tristan has to say.

Tristan nods. "I can prove it. I brought something to show you."

"No," Ada snaps. "It's too late. We're leaving."

In fact, it's time they left New York. Started new somewhere else.

Ada spins around, nursing her anger like armor. She hasn't even taken a step when Eric grabs her arm, stopping her.

"I think we should hear what they have to say."

Ada frowns. Eric's never done something like this. "Let go of me."

Anguish twists his handsome features. "I'm doing this for us," he whispers. "Please, Ada."

She tugs, but he doesn't let go. The flash of anger is as uncontrolled as the bolt of energy that shoots over her skin. Eric grits his teeth, the tendons of his neck standing out in stark relief as the electricity leaps from her body to his.

But he doesn't let go.

Instantly regretting her actions, Ada stops pulling. Her anger dissolves in a blink. And she remains exactly where she is.

"Eric, I'm so sorry," she whispers. Hurting him is something she'd never want to do.

He shakes his head. "Just hear them out," he pleads quietly.

Ada nods. She'd do anything for Eric.

Tristan steps forward, and there's a box in his hands. "There are three stones in here." He grips the lid, his face intense. "If you're a Zodiac, Ada, we'll know."

27

TRISTAN

Tristan has to stop his hands from trembling. If it wasn't for Eric, Ada wouldn't be here right now. They would've lost her.

And now, she's staring at the box as if it's as alien as she is.

Tristan hasn't felt fate resting in the balance like this since when Brielle found her stone. The tourmaline, leaving the tanzanite behind for someone else to claim.

Possibly Ada.

She tears her gaze away from the box and glares at the other Zodiacs beside Tristan. "Tell them to back off."

Tristan doesn't have to say anything. He hears Jareth and Veronica move, then Logan and Cassandra. Brielle is the last to step back, and Tristan almost feels it like a physical tear. She's been so silent since Ada arrived, almost still as a statue. Is this as painful for her as it is him?

Ada's sharp gaze returns to him. "Well? What do I need to do?"

With a fast motion—tearing off the proverbial band aid— Tristan lifts the lid. The three stones inside glitter as they catch the sunlight. The clear diamond on the left, the deep blue of the lapis lazuli nestled to the right…and the royal purple of the tanzanite in the center.

Waiting to be reunited with its other half.

Tristan swallows. "One of these stones is yours. Kept safe until you could be reunited with it."

Ada glances at Eric, her eyes wide. "They're like yours."

Eric blinks, pulling at a cord around his neck. From deep within his shirt, he withdraws a sea-green gem. The turquoise. No wonder Eric's powers were so strong. He's had his stone all along.

"You're the Aquarius," Tristan tells him.

Eric's eyes flash with joy. He presses his other hand to Ada's shoulder. "One of these has got to be yours. It's why you've never been able to control your powers."

Ada lifts her hand, then freezes. "Which one?" she whispers.

"We won't know until you touch them," Tristan responds, his throat tight.

There's no doubt Ada is a Zodiac, and she's about to learn that for herself. It's whether she's the Gemini that they're all about to discover.

"Come on, Ada," Eric encourages in a hushed whisper. "This is what we've been searching for all this time."

Ada looks up at him, her face alive with anticipation. With a quick, sharp movement, she presses her lips to his. "Thank you for insisting I stay."

"Anything for you, Ada," he says huskily. "Always."

Tristan hides his frown at their obvious connection. He knew they were close, but not that close…

Ada visibly swallows as she lifts her hand again. "They're all so pretty," she murmurs.

And one of them is about to come alive in her hand.

Her hand hovers, shifting a little to the right, toward the diamond. But then she stops. Her hand moves left, drawn to the lapis lazuli. The gem is the most beautiful blue Tristan has ever seen. But Ada stops again, a shadow of a frown ghosting her brow. Her breath comes in short bursts, like she's trying to hold it, and yet trying not to hyperventilate at the same time.

The tanzanite rests in the middle, an empty depression beside it.

Her gaze flies to Tristan. "What if it's none of them?"

"You have a stone," he responds with certainty. "You're one of us, Ada. Just like Eric is."

She bites her lip as she blinks rapidly, obviously overcome with emotion. With a quick movement she picks one of the stones.

Tristan's breath disintegrates. She has the tanzanite.

Ada holds it up, pinched between her fingers. If Tristan was planning on breathing anytime soon, he would've found he couldn't. His lungs are frozen, incapable of working. The air around him just solidified, as unmoving as the rest of him.

Ada's eyes widen as she registers what he has. She gasps, lifting the tanzanite higher to show Eric.

Letting him see what just sealed all their fates.

The purple gem is glowing.

Tristan has found his Gemini soulmate.

28

BRIELLE

Ada is the Gemini Twin.

As quietly and invisibly as she can, Brielle slips out away from the group and leaves the cemetery. She can't be here right now. She just has to get out of here.

Once her feet touch the solid surface of the sidewalk that will lead her away from what should be a victorious reunion for all the Zodiacs, she can finally breathe again. But as her lungs regain function, a gaping sore opens and festers in her heart. She feels nothing. Not sorrow, not regret, certainly not joy. The nothing is simultaneously a blessing and a burden.

She should feel something, shouldn't she? Only about a week ago, she was in Tristan's arms, basking under the glow of his kisses, the delicious burn of his touch, the perfect way they seemed to fit together.

As her quick pace carries her away to an uncertain desti-nation, the thought crosses her mind that she should at least feel angry. The only guy she's ever loved has now found his replacement for her, and will never look at her the same way again. If he looks at her at all. His eyes will forever be glued to Ada. That should piss her off, at the very least.

But…nothing.

Nothing but a gaping and steadily growing void where her heart used to be.

Decidedly, she pulls out her phone and texts Kerrim.

Still up for that date?

The only measure of time passing is a breeze that sweeps her brunette locks into her face, and she doesn't even have the care to brush them away. She just reads the text through the thick strands.

I thought you'd never ask. When?

How about right now? she replies.

Ping me your location and I'll pick you up?

She does as he requested and sits on the curb, stuffing her phone into her pocket and staring blankly at the black tar of the road.

This isn't a bad thing, she tells herself. This will tip the balance in the fight against Chardis. They'll win!

Yet no joy at the thought can reach her.

You knew this day would come. You knew it would never be you.

The thought doesn't even cause a sting, only makes the hole inside her grow larger, more ravenous. She may disappear inside it soon. The eventuality almost comforts her, if she could feel such a thing.

As the sunset's orange glow paints everything around her, a car stops in front of Brielle. She looks up. It's Kerrim's black Mustang.

She hears the driver's door open, and soon Kerrim is stooping beside her.

"Hey." His voice takes on a note of concern. "I kinda expected to pick you up at your house, then I find the address you sent me is downwind of a cemetery. You know, if you were trying to run away, you did a shit job."

A dry chuckle escapes her throat.

"Are you okay?" he asks.

She looks up at him, and dammit if he isn't the most tempting thing she's ever seen. His dark eyes promise things she never knew she wanted—excitement, thrill, danger…lostness.

Brielle needs to get lost.

"I will be," she answers. "I've had a really crummy day, and you'd be my savior if you rescued me from it."

A sexy grin spreads across his face. "Well, I wouldn't be a proper knight in shining armor if I didn't rescue a damsel in distress. Hop in." He stands and opens the front passenger door for her.

Gratefully, and a bit too excitedly, she climbs into the car, and he gets into the driver's seat.

"So, my lady, where to?" The way he holds her gaze has her insides melting.

She very much wants to melt, to let go of everything. To forget.

"Surprise me," she finds herself saying, truly meaning it.

His lips curve into an impish smile. "As you wish, my lady."

He pulls into the street with vigor, and the vibrating roar of his engine is a welcome whole-body distraction. She can feel the hum rattle her bones, and it's sheer elation. Something that takes no conscious thought, triggers no emotional reaction, it's purely physical, and she loves it!

"How fast can this puppy go?" she asks, a hint of her inner thrill-seeker in her voice.

He gives her a wry, sidelong glance. "You really wanna find out?"

She nods eagerly.

In response, he smiles and shifts the clutch into the next gear, speeding down the road.

They're going faster than she's ever experienced before as

a passenger, and it's invigorating! With each pop of the clutch, each spike of the speedometer, her pulse hikes into higher and higher gear. Brielle dives into every too-sharp turn, revels in every embellished straightaway, relishing the ambitiously reaching dials on the dashboard.

Kerrim somehow steers them onto a swerving mountainside road that hugs the coastline, revving the engine to push them to dangerous speeds as they round the curves. But Brielle feels no fear. Caution has gone out the window, which she welcomely rolls down to let the wicked breeze whip at her hair and face. She hopes the lashings give her battle scars. Doesn't she need some reminder badge of honor for falling for Tristan before he met his match?

She swipes her hair away with a vengeance at the idea and sticks her head out the open window, inviting the wind to recreate the map of her face, to give her a new mask that could hide the damage this day has wrought.

They continue swerving and speeding without a word, the thrill slowly closing the hole in Brielle's chest and creating a new throbbing desire for risk. For mayhem. For anything that will erase the memory of how it felt to be in Tristan's arms.

After an hour of cliff-trailing fun, they stop at the top of a rocky hill where a parking lot of gravel beckons them toward a lighthouse.

Kerrim parks the car, indicating toward the sign for a restaurant on the front of the building. "I found this place about a week ago. I figured it would be a nice surprise for you."

He jumps out and rushes around to open her door, but she's in no mood for that depth of chivalry, so she opens it herself and stands, ready to face this new adventure. She's a Zodiac Guardian, for pitch sake. She can open her own door.

Kerrim doesn't miss a beat as she escorts herself, just

readjusts his manner to her level and walks alongside her up to the entrance.

"This place has the best Maine lobster anywhere in the country," he says. "I'd stake my reputation as a scoundrel on it." He winks at her, and dammit if she can't fight the blush from rising.

Though she knows he's joking, she has no doubt he's a scoundrel. But secretly, she knows that's exactly what she wants right now. Someone to darken the glow Tristan has had on her life.

"How did you find this place?" she asks as they approach the hostess counter.

"A beast like mine needs room to roam. I found this road, and this lighthouse just happened to be at the top. It serves as a perfect meal to end any day, especially the worst of them." He gives a single reassuring nod, letting her know he realizes she's struggling, and promising that somehow, this meal will fix it all.

The hostess returns to her podium, spouts a bunch of words about specials that Brielle doesn't hear, then ushers them to their seats overlooking a breathtaking cliff-side view over the water. Brielle loves hearing the waves crash over the rocks below, loves seeing the ocean span out to the horizon.

She's only recently realized how massive the Universe is, but at this moment, she appreciates how vast the Earth is in its own right.

"So...what happened?" Kerrim asks in a chocolatey tone that makes her ache to spill all her secrets.

She has to look away from his enticing gaze lest she do just that.

"That guy, Tristan," she begins, looking down at her fiddling fingers, and already hating the taste of the words she's yet to speak. "He...started dating someone else."

His dark brows flare in a surprised frown. "I meant, what happened at the shipping yard, but wow!"

"Oh," she says, feeling embarrassed. Of course he'd be wondering what happened with that whole mess. Somehow, not being chosen over a stranger by her best friend ranks miles above being trapped by an FBI most wanted lawyer and then being interrogated by those FBI agents who captured him.

She really needs to reconsider her priorities.

"Um." She doesn't want to lie to him, but how is she supposed to explain that whole cluster fudge? "That turned out to be a real mess."

"I had offered to stay with you," he hedges.

She nods. "Actually, I'm glad you didn't."

He leans back into his chair and cocks his head, truly intrigued. "Why is that?"

"It…" She weighs her words heavily. She doesn't want to scare him off. "Turned out to be a lot of trouble. I'd really rather not get into it."

He shrugs. "Fair enough." His eyes narrow and his brow flares. "I knew you were a woman of mystery."

As the blush rages in Brielle's cheeks, the waiter comes to take their order. Kerrim orders a round of fresh caught lobster for both of them, and soon they're alone again.

He turns his delving gaze back to her. "Any way I can coax some of that mystery out of you?"

She purses her lips. She knows she has to be careful. "Depends. I'll warn you, I don't lie. But if you ask a question I can't answer honestly, I won't answer at all."

His brow raises in a refreshingly surprised look, and he nods. "I like that. The mystery deepens."

He leans forward, his arms crossed over the table, and grills her with an interrogating gaze that forces her to look away.

"Why were you at the shipping yard?" he asks.

The compulsive urge to vomit the truth grips her, but she reins it in, gathering her words before she speaks them. "My apparently former employer had less than scrupulous ventures in mind for me."

She can't meet his gaze, or she knows she'll be unable to hide the rest of the truth.

"Are you hurt?"

"No," she replies instinctively. At least, not from that encounter. Not physically, anyway. She's incredibly lucky to make it out of Jack Cadbury's grasp without issue, that's for sure.

Kerrim nods, accepting. "Good." He looks her over slowly. "Are you...in trouble?"

She takes a minute to debate before replying. "I don't think so?" It comes out as more of a question, which has Kerrim furrowing his brow.

He glances at his untouched glass of water. "Do you want to keep talking about this?"

Her head shakes before she can stop it.

"I see." He frowns, thinking about something she can't anticipate. Then his eyes return to hers. "You say that you can't lie. And I believe you. I can't help but wonder, how did that come about?"

She opens her mouth, then pauses as she realizes she doesn't have a real answer. She's always assumed it was because of the guilt that came from lying, from holding onto the lies of others. But him asking the question now makes her realize it's a choice.

She could have easily swallowed the guilt of it, learned like everyone else to deal with it, and lied to get her way. But not lying is a choice. She has chosen, repeatedly, not to add more to her plate. And she still stands by that choice.

Brielle swallows. "It was ingrained into me at a young age

not to lie. I've seen the damage lies can cost people, especially as an orphan—"

He chokes on his water mid-sip. "You're an orphan?"

She blanches at the miscommunication. "Well, not anymore. I was recently adopted by the best parents." One of which is currently incarcerated for a crime he didn't commit, she adds internally.

"Wow, I'm…so sorry," he stammers.

"Don't be." She shrugs. "That's life for some of us."

He swallows his sip of water and purses his lips. "The truth is, I would have been, too. Not in the same way, but my dad had a sort of…crisis that almost took him away from me. Now every day that he's with me, I thank the powers that be that it didn't."

A frown crinkles her forehead as she gets a glimpse at a pain he's trying to hide. "I'm glad for you. No one deserves to have their family taken away."

He nods, stoic for a silent moment. Then his expression returns to an impish one, and he looks up at her. "So, on to the Tristan of it all?"

She scoffs and shakes her head. "I'd just like to forget all of that, please." She looks out to the swaying seas, hoping to find solace in their ever changing monotony.

She feels the spotlight of his eyes move away from her. "I can understand that. Believe it or not, there are plenty of things I'd like to forget, too." The weight of his glance moves back to her, and she's helpless not to meet it. "Maybe we can help each other forget."

As soon as she does, their faces meet halfway over the table, their lips pressing against each other's.

They kiss like that, tongues tangling and getting lost in each other until the waiter interrupts them. Brielle flushes, but Kerrim dismisses the food with a couple twenties and whisks her out of the restaurant and back to his car, where they continue to make out.

And for one blissful moment, Brielle doesn't have a care in the world.

Forget about Chardis.

Forget about the turmoil in the Universe.

Forget that Tristan has his soulmate.

29

TRISTAN

"I'm a Zodiac," Ada shouts, turning to Eric to show him the glowing purple stone with the same excitement as a child on Christmas Day. One who just got everything she wished for.

"I never doubted it for a second," he whoops.

Ada launches at him, but Eric's arms are already open. She lands against his chest and he spins her around, her red curls billowing out. They laugh breathlessly, faces close as they gaze into each other's eyes.

When they finally stop, they kiss, pressing their lips together as if the action is a promise. Their happiness is like a freaking supernova, it's so bright.

Eric pulls back. "Ouch," he says, his voice light with humor.

Ada's eyes shine. "That won't be a problem for much longer."

Tristan looks away. His throat feels like a boa constrictor has wrapped around it. He never imagined that when he found his soulmate he'd feel so...conflicted. That he'd struggle to say the words out loud. He looks around, registering that Brielle's gone. He's not surprised. Maybe it's easier without her here.

He notes the way the other Zodiacs are all standing still, glancing at each other. They're also aware this should be a celebration…

"So," Ada says, looking at Tristan and then the others. "Eric filled me in on who is who, so give me the low down. Can I fly?"

Tristan clears his throat. "Why don't we go back to HQ so we can talk? We can't afford to be overheard."

"Excellent idea," Ada says chirpily. She takes Eric's hand. "We'll follow you."

Avoiding the gaze of the others, Tristan makes his way to his truck. He leads the convoy of Zodiacs that drive back to the house. Jareth and Veronica behind him, Logan and Cassandra in the next car, then Ada and Eric in an old rust bucket.

The whole way there, his mind is on a loop.

Ada's his soulmate.

And yet she's obviously with Eric.

And Tristan's feelings for Brielle haven't changed. A little part of him hoped they would fade, maybe disappear altogether, when his Gemini Twin appeared. But Ada's here, and his heart still feels like it's been crushed by King Kong on a rampage.

He reaches the house and waits for the others to join him out the front. "This is our headquarters, but Jareth and I also live here," he tells Ada and Eric. "It was left to me by a guy called Alden, he followed us here to help the Zodiacs, but was killed not long after he found me."

Ada takes a step back, taking in the large building that's the love child of a manor and a fortress. "How many bedrooms?"

"Twelve," Tristan answers, for the first time realizing

Alden probably intended for the Zodiacs to live all under one roof.

Ada glances at Eric and he raises his eyebrows. "No more sleeping in a car," he says in wonder.

Hearing that two Zodiacs have been sleeping rough has Tristan suppressing a frown. Despite his typhoon-level turmoil, he's glad these two will have somewhere safe and comfortable to live.

He passes his hand over the sensor and Ada whistles. "I think I might've liked this Alden."

"Wait till you see HQ then," says Cassandra, a hint of pride in her voice.

Tristan leads the way in. "I'll give you a tour of the house later on and you can choose your bedrooms."

Ada loops her arm through Eric's. "We'll only need one," she says with a cheeky grin.

Eric flushes but doesn't correct her, trying unsuccessfully to hide his joy.

Veronica and Jareth glance at each other, but Tristan pretends he doesn't notice. He's not sure this could score any higher on the crap meter.

He walks through the living room to the bookcase that hides the staircase to the lower level. "For now, we'll show you HQ."

He moves the photo of Zarius and Tess, also unable to look at them. Zarius dreamed of the moment they'd find the Gemini Twin. Tess always had faith that it would happen.

Well, now it's here and Tristan's incapable of celebrating. They never considered there would be a cost to uniting the Gemini Twins, let alone that it would be so high.

The bookcase slides silently open, revealing the stairs.

"Now that's cool," says Eric.

Tristan leads them down then steps aside, letting the others in. Jareth tries to catch Tristan's eye as he steps past, but Tristan pretends to be fascinated with his shoes. Seems there's a spot of what looks like Bolognese sauce on one. His gut clenches so tight it makes it hard to breathe. The Bolognese Brielle made for them a few days ago.

"Whoa," Ada says in awe. She moves from one computer to another, simultaneously taking in the screens up on the wall. "This is some pretty advanced tech you've got here."

"Except we don't know how to use most of it," says Logan.

Ada grins at him. "You will now."

Eric walks over to wrap an arm around her shoulder. "You'll probably upgrade the whole thing while you're there."

"I was going to let them see the awesomeness when I was done."

Eric chuckles. "Sorry," he says, not sounding the least apologetic. He's obviously proud of her.

Ada looks at the four people in the room with her. "So, Eric filled me in on everyone's powers and that butthead, Chardis. But who is what Zodiac sign?" She grips her hand tighter, and Tristan knows she's holding the tanzanite.

Jareth raises his hand. "Capricorn."

"Taurus," says Logan.

Cassandra juts out a hip. "I'm the Leo."

Veronica smiles impishly. "I'm a Taurus like my brother, but that's probably beside the point seeing as I'm human."

"Brielle's the Libra, but she had somewhere to be," Tristan says, focusing on keeping his voice steady. "And I'm a Gemini."

Eric's eyes light up with recognition. He turns to Ada. "Remember how I told you he has a twin out there, somewhere?"

"Oh yes." She beams up at Eric. "Everyone should find their soulmate in their lifetime."

Jareth clears his throat as Cassandra coughs delicately. Logan and Veronica look at Tristan pointedly.

He needs to tell her.

"So," Ada says, clearly excited. "If Eric's the Aquarius, that leaves Sagittarius, Aries, Pisces, Scorpio and Cancer." She opens her hand to reveal the tanzanite. "Which one am I?"

The room falls silent and the air suddenly feels too thick to breathe. Tristan reaches into his shirt and withdraws his own gem.

The other tanzanite.

"Ada," he starts, finding himself faltering. In all the times he imagined saying these words, he never thought he'd hesitate. That he'd selfishly wish they weren't true. "You're the other Gemini. You're my soulmate."

30

ADA

A da's conscious she doesn't move for long seconds.

She's the Gemini?

She's Tristan's soulmate?

How the hell is that even possible?

A choked sound beside her, one she's never heard Eric make, snaps her out of her stupor. "No. You've made a mistake."

Tristan tries to smile, but the motion dies before it is even born. "The stone you have. It's the tanzanite. You're the second Gemini, Ada." He holds up his own gem.

It's identical to the one she's holding.

"Like hell she is," shouts Eric. He steps past Ada and shoves Tristan. "Ada and I belong together."

Tristan doesn't fight Eric off, simply rights himself as he holds Eric's gaze. "Believe me, I know the feeling."

Ada rushes forward, putting her hand on Eric's arm. "I'm sure this is a misunderstanding. I'm with you, no one else."

Her words make Tristan wince. "This is far too important to be a mix up."

Eric seems to inflate, as if he's filling with fury. "No!"

"There has to be another way," says Ada, conscious of the strong vein of pleading in her voice. Maybe if she's the Gemini, it doesn't mean being tied to Tristan for the rest of her life. "Surely the Zodiac power is enough to defeat this Chardis.

Her chest aches. Please let there be another way.

"Chardis killed my parents," says Tristan, his own pain flashing across his face. "He crushed their hearts before my eyes and there was nothing I could do."

"And he killed mine, too," adds Jareth. "He burned them alive."

Veronica moves closer to him and clasps his hand. "We almost died in similar circumstances."

Cassandra shifts uncomfortably. "He sent an asteroid to collide with Earth."

"And then there's the wormhole," says Logan. "Who knows what he's planning next."

Tristan straightens. "When the Gemini Twins are united, their power will be the greatest the Universe has ever seen," he says quietly, obviously quoting something or someone. "It is as good as Chardis is evil. It is the light to his night. It is the one thing he fears."

The words are a prophecy.

A vow.

The promise of how they can win.

Ada's once again frozen. Cold right down to her marrow. The only thing that betrays her agitation is the buzz of electricity dancing over her skin. She glances down as her palm opens, almost as if it belongs to someone else.

The tanzanite is glowing again.

She is the second Gemini.

The same strangled sound is torn from Eric. She spins to look at him, lost as to how she can make this right.

His beautiful face is pale and strained. "You're the one

who fought for this," he says through whitewashed lips. "You wouldn't stop until you found out the truth."

Ada blinks. "No," she says hoarsely. "This was never what I wanted."

"Is it because you knew?" He takes a step back, even more color draining from his cheeks. "You were searching for your...soulmate?" He whispers the last word, as if it's filtered through pain.

"No! That was never what I was doing! You know I love you."

Eric stumbles back several more steps. "Well, you got what you wanted, Ada. Answers."

He spins on his heel and lurches toward the stairs. Logan moves to get out of the way, but still reaches out to try and steady Eric. But Eric jerks away, almost slamming into the opposite wall.

"Stay the hell away from me. All of you."

Ada takes a step toward him, but he's gone, running up the stairs two at a time. A few seconds later, there's the soft thud of a door slamming.

Silence echoes through the room. Suddenly, the technology that was so exciting a few minutes ago, hums hollowly. The people she'd considered moving in with feel like strangers. Worse. They've taken away the one thing that mattered to her.

Eric.

Tristan holds out a hand. "For what it's worth, I'm really sorry."

Except it makes no difference. She crumples into the nearest chair. "What have I done?" she whispers brokenly.

Eric's right. She wanted this. He tried to talk her out of it, but she railroaded him over and over again. She wanted for them to be a real couple so badly, she failed to consider that she'd tear them apart.

And now he's gone. He just walked straight out of her life.

What's more, she broke his heart.

She shoots to her feet. "I have to go after him."

"I'm not sure that's a good idea," Veronica says gently. "He's hurting."

Jareth looks at Ada, his dark gaze full of compassion. "And there's nothing you can do to change what you are."

The Gemini Twin.

Tristan rubs his forehead, looking pained. "Maybe he needs some time. To accept this."

A millennium could pass and this wouldn't be okay. It will never be something Eric can accept.

"He'll see that we've all had to make sacrifices," Tristan adds, his voice raspy.

Cassandra crosses her arms. "Unless he doesn't come back," she says under her breath.

But everyone in the room heard it.

Ada's heart cracks and constricts simultaneously. Eric can disappear without a trace. He knows how to, seeing as they've been doing it half their lives.

She has to go after him. She has to make this right.

Before she can move, Tristan's cell phone rings, the sound strident in the emotion laden room. He glances at the screen and his face tightens. "It's Brielle."

He takes a few steps away and turns his back. "Hey, you okay?"

The softness in his voice is unmistakable. For the first time, Ada wonders why she's not here. Shouldn't Brielle have been here to welcome the next two Zodiacs into their tight knit little family?

Ada glances away. It's probably a good thing. Brielle didn't have to witness the train wreck that just happened.

Tristan's spine stiffens. "It's what?"

The four others in the room are instantly on high alert. They all contract, faces full of concern.

"Yep, we'll meet you there." Tristan's about to hang up when he stops. "And Brielle, stay safe."

Jamming his cell back in his pocket, Tristan raises troubled eyes to the team. Although Ada's only just met him, she knows something's happened. Something bad.

"It's Grace Orphanage. It's on fire."

Cassandra gasps. "No. Sister Agnes, the nuns." Her eyes widen. "The children."

"That's why we're rolling out," he says grimly.

The other four are already moving, rushing toward the stairs.

But Ada shakes her head as she stays where she is. "It's obvious it's a trap. Chardis is trying to draw you out."

"Draw *us* out," Logan says quietly.

Ada almost flinches as he corrects her. If she's part of the Zodiacs, then she loses Eric.

Tristan shrugs, suggesting he's already considered her suggestion. "There's a good chance this is exactly what you say—a trap. If Chardis knows several of the Zodiacs came from Grace Orphanage, he's banking that we'll run to save it." He shrugs. "But we don't have a choice. We have to help if we can."

He's right, dammit. They're talking the lives of innocent women and children. She can't turn her back on that, no matter which Zodiac she is.

As they all run up the stairs, she feels her chest rip and tears sting her eyes.

Eric will disappear.

Taking her heart with him.

31

BRIELLE

*N*o, this can't be happening!

The devastation at the sight of Brielle's long-time home is overwhelming. Fire paints the evening sky an angry orange that bleeds to red before blackening into heady smoke. Screams of women and children are a morbid chorus as all race to escape.

Not long after climbing into the car to make out, Kerrim had suddenly been needed elsewhere but had agreed to take her home. She'd seen the flames on the way and demanded he let her out. He'd clearly looked conflicted, debating whether to obey or get her to safety. But she'd made it clear she could handle herself, and that these people needed her. Honestly, she'd have jumped out of the moving Mustang if she'd needed to. Finally and reluctantly, Kerrim had pulled over, wishing he could stay to help but promising to call the authorities as he continued on to where he was needed.

She didn't care that he couldn't stay to help, her own urgency to do so had the reins. But the ensuing bitterness at the realization that Tristan would have stayed no matter what clung to her consciousness as she ran toward the burning building.

Tristan. He would want to know. She calls him as she continues forward, knowing the orphanage needs more than just her help. It needs the Zodiacs.

"Hey, you okay?" he asks. His voice is steady, but she can hear the steel in it.

"Tristan! The orphanage!" she pants as she reaches the steps. "It's on fire!"

"It's what?" he exclaims.

"The whole thing is up in flames," she continues. "They need our help! Now!"

"Yep, we'll meet you there," he says. Before she hangs up, she hears him say, "And Brielle, stay safe."

How is it that those small words of caring still warm her heart?

She shakes it off, the heat of the flames basting her skin.

"Brielle?" Sister Lori gapes at her as she carries out a crying child in each arm.

"What happened?" Brielle asks, hands fluttering toward the children, ready to assist.

"I-I-I don't know," the nun stutters, rushing down the steps. "The whole place just suddenly went up in flames. I have no idea where it started. It seemed to start everywhere all at once."

Skins. The accusation echoes in Brielle's mind.

"How many are still inside?" she asks.

Sister Lori's heart visibly breaks, her face nearly cracking in two. "Most of the older kids are already out, but—oh, Brielle, the nursery!" Tears stream down her desperate face.

All the babies are still inside.

"Where's Sister Agatha?" Brielle demands.

"The nursery," Sister Lori says forebodingly.

Brielle's hands ball into determined fists. "Get those kids

to safety. The firefighters should be here soon." She bursts into the burning doorway without waiting for a response, flames licking at her bare forearms and ankles.

But she runs in so quickly, their lashing doesn't have time to stick, only singing the frayed ends of her jean capris.

The inside of the orphanage looks even worse than the outside. Blazes cover every wall and blanket the ceiling, and the smoke that fills the air burns her lungs, forcing coughs up her throat. She realizes she's no good to anyone this vulnerable. She needs her suit.

Taking a quick glance around, she notes that no one is in view of the entryway, then whispers *"Akash"* as she makes a mad dash for the hallway, erupting into her suit mid-sprint. As soon as the alien enamel covers her face, she can breathe clearly and easily, and her eyes are no longer hindered by the sting of the smoke.

The nursery is up the stairs around the corner. As she runs toward it, she quickly scans each room as she passes them, praying she won't find anyone hunkering down inside. Luckily, each one appears empty, and she silently thanks pitch every time she continues on to the next.

She's finally made it to the last room on the right before the stairs. It appears empty. Brielle leaps for the staircase, but a soft whimper cuts through the crackling like a knife through butter. She jumps backward and inspects the room more closely.

A message darts across the inside of her visor.

Lifeform detected.

Oh pitch, there's someone in here!

"Hello?" she calls out, hoping they can hear her through the suit.

Sniffle, sniffle. "Yes? I'm here?" responds a small, frightened voice. A figure peeks out from behind the bedpost, and Brielle recognizes her instantly.

Marie. One of the Brady Bunch girls. The one who always bullied her the most. And she looks positively terrified.

Brielle shoots out a hand. "Please, you have to come with me."

Marie eyes her for a moment, sniffling all the while. "You're one of *them,* aren't you?"

Suddenly, a beam above their heads cracks in half, barely managing to remain on the ceiling.

"Now!" Brielle shouts, and Marie automatically jumps out from behind the bed and runs to take Brielle's open hand.

Palms clasped tightly, the two sprint for the exit. Marie trips over a splintered floorboard, and in her desperation, Brielle scoops her up and carries her the rest of the way out. Marie has her hands gripped tightly around Brielle's neck, and she feels like a tiny bird in her arms.

The entry hall is, impossibly, even more swollen with angry red, and Brielle protectively envelops Marie with her suited arms as she leaps through the front doors. Marie intakes a sharp breath once they're in open air, and Brielle sets her gently on the sidewalk past the steps.

"Thank you," Marie says. As Brielle turns to dash back inside, Marie's grip tightens on Brielle's hand, making her pause. "Your secret is safe with me…Brielle…"

Brielle gasps. But there's no time to deal with this now, neither verbally nor mentally. She has more to do.

Without a response, she springs back inside, this time heading straight for the stairs. Sister Agatha and the babies are more important.

She takes the stairs three steps at time, hopping up them as quickly as she can. Once on the second floor, she darts for the nursery.

To her horror, every crib harbors a wailing infant. Sister Agatha is here, hoisting a third baby into her already over-burdened arms.

"Sister, you have to get out!" Brielle shrieks.

Sister Agatha turns, her eyes only slightly flaring with alarm at the appearance of a suited figure. "I'm not leaving my charges," she states passionately.

Brielle grits her teeth. "Go, now! I've got them."

Sister Agatha darts out of the room with her armload of babes, and Brielle hoists as many as she can into her embrace. Out of the corner of her eye, she sees another figure. She turns.

"Eric?" she blurts, recognizing the handsome blond instantly. Her vizor goes down, showing her face. "What are you doing here?"

"I saw the flames and I had to help," he says gruffly.

A thousand questions enter her mind, but she has no time to acknowledge them. All she can say is, "Thank you."

He nods curtly, then rushes out with a couple of screeching infants, and she's quick on his tail. They leap onto the sidewalk, a puff of smoke pushing them out, and a multitude of hands eagerly take their charges from them.

Brielle's head whips around in search of Sister Agatha. Only to see her leap back into the building at the last second.

"No!" Brielle screams.

As fast as she can, she rushes back in after her. Why would Sister Agatha go back? Brielle's here now, far more capable for this than she is. She doesn't need to do this!

By the grace of the god she so deeply believes in, Sister Agatha beats Brielle up the stairs and back into the nursery. When Brielle reaches the room, the nun is already trying to hoist another child out of its crib.

"Sister, you have to *leave!*" Brielle shrieks the last word with as much urgency as she can inflect.

"I can't leave them!" Sister Agatha says resolutely, tears streaming down her face.

"You don't have to," Brielle says, placing a reassuring hand on the Sister's arm. "I told you, I've got them."

Sister Agatha looks at her for a short yet impossibly long moment, debating. Finally, she nods, then turns for the door. Relief washes over Brielle.

"Ahh!" The blood-curdling scream reaches Brielle's suit-enhanced senses too late. By the time Brielle spins around, Sister Agatha's midsection is trapped by a heavy and blazing fallen beam.

"No!" Brielle cries, rushing to her side.

Acting on autopilot, Brielle heaves the smoldering chunk of wood off her, only to realize that one of the large splinters has speared deeply into Sister Agatha's abdomen. Her face is scrunched in pain, a deep, gritting sound puffing out of her in frenzied pants.

"No!" Brielle screams again, gripping the splinter.

"Don't!" calls a familiar voice, and soon Eric is hovering beside them. "If you pull it out, she'll only die faster."

"Die?" The word feels foreign on her tongue. No. No. No. Sister Agatha *can't* die! It's just not possible. It can't happen.

She looks back down at Sister Agatha's face. Only to realize that her vizor is still down.

Pitch!

How could she be so careless?

But the way Sister Agatha is looking at her right now is… there are no words for it. The nun's eyes are welling with tears, glistening in the sunset glow of the greedy fire that surrounds them.

A croak forces its way out of Brielle's throat, one that stems from deep inside her soul.

Sister Agatha's hand is suddenly clutching hers, but there's no fear or sadness in her moist eyes.

Only pride, and love deeper than the deepest crevice of the ocean.

"Hush, my child," Sister Agatha croons softly between

pants. "Don't cry for me." She pats Brielle's hand with her other hand. "Just save the babies."

Suddenly, Sister Agatha sighs, and Brielle can almost see the pain leaving her face, the wrinkles smoothing into an expression of contentment. Stricken, Brielle snaps her head at Eric, who nods.

He's taken her pain away.

Gratitude overwhelms her, more powerful than she's ever known, and she knows she'll forever be in his debt for this. Tears burst from her eyes and flow like rivers down her face.

The only mother she's ever truly known, the woman who raised her with endless compassion and without bias, is dying.

Sister Agatha's other hand comes up to pat Brielle's hand on hers. "I always knew you'd be someone great."

A rattle reverberates through the nun's chest and up her throat, making its final debut weakly through her lips.

And then no more.

Sorrow stabs through Brielle's chest like the splinter that stole Sister Agatha from her, and she expels it out loudly, the sound deafening all others.

A hand pats Brielle's shoulder as they heave in agony, and the wail silences with a hiccup as she turns to him. "We have to finish what she started," he says softly, looking up at the cribs.

Sharply inhaling and smothering the cries that beg to be set free, Brielle rises, closes her visor, and gathers the rest of the babies with Eric's help. Together, they flee the building as it further collapses.

Though he and Brielle saved the infants, and all the orphans are safe, except for a few burns here and there, she failed.

She failed the woman who raised her.

Sister Agatha is dead.

32

TRISTAN

Tristan's running, frantically scanning the chaos as he approaches the blazing orphanage. "Brielle!" he shouts. "Where are you?"

The crowd parts and she rises from where she was kneeling beside the still form of a woman. "Tristan," she says brokenly.

He doesn't stop until he's engulfed her in a hug, wrapping his arms around her and making sure she's alright. She's soot streaked and tear stained, but she seems unhurt.

She presses her face into his chest, her hands twisting his shirt. "Sister Agatha, she's…"

It's then that he sees it's the matron of the orphanage lying on the grass, her face serene, but her chest unmoving. Blood stains the front of her prim blouse.

"She was saving all the children in the nursery," Brielle hiccups. "I helped her. But…she didn't make it."

"I'm so sorry, Bri. I know what she meant to you."

Sister Agatha was the only maternal figure Brielle had throughout most of her life.

Brielle buries her face in tighter, sobs racking her shoulders. For long seconds, she feels too fragile for all of this. Protectiveness wells within Tristan, quickly followed by a wave of hatred. Chardis did this, he knows it.

He's the one who keeps taking those closest to them.

The wailing of sirens pierces the crackling air and a paramedic rushes over and kneels beside Sister Agatha. A quick check tells the woman what Tristan and Brielle already know.

She's dead.

The paramedic calls for a blanket and Tristan leads Brielle a few steps away. He finds the other Zodiacs there, faces grief stricken and shocked. Cassandra has her hand over her mouth as she stares at the angry, growing flames, and Logan wraps his arm around her shoulder. Not far away stand the sobbing nuns and the confused tears of the children. Black plumes of smoke pour into the sky, tainting it with ash.

A firefighter comes up beside them. "Is everyone out?" he shouts.

One of the nuns steps forward. "I just did a head count, yes. We're all here."

Relief courses through Tristan. He tightens his arms around Brielle. "You saved a lot of people today."

She sniffs. "But not Sister Agatha."

"You tried, and that's all you can do."

The firefighter makes some signals to the other emergency personnel swarming around, then turns back to the nun. "Good, because no one could go in there and come out alive."

Tristan turns back to take in the old building. There's a *boom* and the flames roar higher, a shower of sparks rising into the blackening sky.

"Parts of the roof are collapsing," mutters the fireman. He

turns to the accumulating crowd, shouting, "We need everyone to get back!"

Tristan keeps his arm around Brielle as they shuffle back, the Zodiacs coming with them, all holding each other. Veronica is murmuring something to Jareth, while Logan is stroking Cassandra's hair. Ada's alone, though, her arms wrapped around her middle. Tristan realizes she spent some of her years here, too.

And it's her—his Gemini Twin—he should be comforting, not Brielle.

Chardis may have failed in drawing out the Zodiacs this time, but they can't defeat him without both the Geminis. Tristan can't forget that, no matter how right Brielle feels in his arms.

He loosens them, clenching his gut as he prepares to step back. They should get back anyway, there's nothing more they can do here.

"Oliver, no!" one of the nuns cries out.

Tristan turns in time to see a boy of about ten break away from the group and run straight toward the burning building. The nun rushes after him only to be grabbed by a firefighter. She struggles and screams as the boy disappears into the orphanage.

"Gear up, people!" shouts the firefighter. "Get your breathing apparatus on!"

The firefighters become a flurry of movement as doors on the truck are opened and closed. They move quickly, trained to do this as fast as possible, no doubt knowing time is of the essence.

But the Zodiacs can move faster.

Tristan glances at Brielle and she nods. They break into a run simultaneously, the others right behind them. He hears Jareth shout to Veronica to stay where she is.

The front door's still open from when the boy went

through. Tristan finds himself in the foyer of the old building. Flames ravage all the walls, skimming over the ceiling with insatiable hunger. One inhale and smoke coats Tristan's lungs.

"Suits!" he shouts, a second later deploying his own. "Akash."

The moment he's enclosed, his vision sharpens and he can breathe again. There's a movement ahead and he sees the young boy dart from behind a counter. The kid glances over his shoulder, flashing a grin, before slipping through another door.

Brielle's gasp echoes through their coms. "He just went straight out the back door."

The smile. The hasty exit.

Pitch. "It's a trap!"

Tristan's just spinning around when there's a *bang*. A man's behind them and he just slammed the door shut. Another man shoves an antique cupboard of some sort across it, something the average person couldn't do.

Skins.

"Tristan," Logan says in a low voice.

A quick scan reveals more Skins materializing from doorways and from behind furniture. Far more than should be here. They were waiting for Zodiacs. In a freaking blazing building.

Now, that's commitment.

There's another *bang*, then a *thud*. Tristan suspects those are the other doors and exits. The Zodiacs won't be getting out easily, nor will the firefighters be coming in any time soon.

He spins around, seeing the other Zodiacs are in their suits. All except Ada.

"Call your suit, Ada!" Tristan shouts. "Hold your stone and say Akash!"

"Tristan!"

Brielle's voice has him spinning around just as a Skin ploughs into his chest. He's shoved backward, slamming into a display case. Glass shatters and timber explodes as he digs his heels in, stopping the Skin from knocking him over. The Skin batters him with punches, but Tristan does the same. And he has a suit to protect him.

One solid hit to the jaw and the Skin is dispatched, but before Tristan can draw a breath, another is on him. Then another.

And another.

"There are too many!" Jareth shouts.

As Tristan deflects and parries, he sees Jareth duck then throw an imaginary fireball at the Skin attacking him. The Skin side steps, giving Jareth the opening he needs. He leaps forward with a kick, one of his favorite moves. He's never been much of a fan of close combat.

Except another Skin behind Jareth leaps, knowing he can't see him.

"Jare—"

A blazing ball of light hits the Skin between his shoulder blades and he falls to the ground, convulsing as smoke from his back joins the rest heading for the ceiling.

"Good job, Cassandra!"

"I can't use them too much," she cries, swinging a round-house as another Skin attacks her. "This place is about to collapse."

Although Tristan can barely feel the flames, he can hear them. They rage at being contained; they roar their intent to destroy. A fireball hitting a wall at just the right spot could bring this whole place down.

A fist ploughs into his helmet, followed by a volley of several more. Tristan's head snaps back with each one, sending pain jolting down his neck. He crouches low and sweeps his leg out. The Skin tumbles to the ground. A second later a section of roof falls onto him, alive with flames.

Tristan turns away as screams fill the air, his stomach churning.

"Zodiac scum!" shouts another Skin, running at him, and Tristan begins the strike and block process all over again.

"Logan, how are they feeling?" he pants between blows.

"There's a sense of urgency." Logan grunts and there's the sound of a body hitting the ground. "They know they don't have much time."

"Amp it up," Tristan orders. "The more desperate they are, the more mistakes they'll make."

"Can do."

In a blink, the Skins become a frenzy. They throw blows as if they have endless energy, they scream their soulless need for Zodiac blood. Two run at Brielle and she quickly steps out of the way at the last second. The Skins plough into each other with a sickening *crunch*.

"Where's Ada?" Tristan asks. A quick scan of the smoky area reveals no second purple suit. "Ada!"

But there's no response through the coms.

Tristan runs several steps in the direction he last saw her, only to face three more Skins. Despite taking so many out, it's as if there's a never-ending supply of them. Like they had some secret breeding program deep in the walls of the orphanage.

Waiting for this moment.

One Skin has a length of timber, and she swings it at Tristan's torso, her smoke-streaked face contorted in hatred. He leaps back, losing some of the distance he just covered.

"You'll die in here!" he shouts at her.

Her lips twist. "Taking you with us will be worth it."

Pitch. By increasing their desperation, they've also multiplied the Skins' determination.

She swings again and Tristan ducks, now on the defensive. "Ada!" he tries one more time through the coms.

No answer.

As he throws up his arm to block the length of wood and it smashes against his suit, he winces. The reverberation through his suit was more than he expected, but he was also struck by a thought.

What if Ada's hurt? Or worse... He mentally shakes himself. Wouldn't he know if something had happened to her?

There's a *creak* and a *groan* and a beam crashes to the floor behind Tristan, sending a flurry of sparks into the smoky air. The Skins attacking him lift their arms to shield their eyes, and Tristan uses the opportunity to plough through all three of them, sending them skittering like bowling pins.

"Get to the center of the room!" he calls to the others.

Away from the blazing walls, where they can work as one.

The Zodiacs progressively work at coming together in the center of the burning foyer. Jareth throws another fireball, but this Skin walks straight through it. She's realized they're little more than an illusion. Brielle executes a flying kick, one the Skin never sees coming, and Chardis's thug is out of commission.

They slowly move in, the smoke getting thicker and thicker, making the Skins cough. Tristan can now feel the heat of the flames even through his suit, and a trickle of sweat skitters down his spine. A message flashes across his visor.

Temperature increasing to extreme levels.

"No kidding," mutters Logan.

"We have to get out of here!" says Cassandra.

She's right. The orphanage is collapsing, and they're surrounded by Skins. "We need to find Ada first."

He frantically scans the room now that he's in the center,

and he finally sees her. She's standing in the back corner, the flames leaping behind her and making her red hair look almost alive.

She's not wearing her suit.

And she's trapped.

Two Skins are closing in on her.

33

ADA

A da grips the tanzanite so hard it hurts. "Akash," she whispers hoarsely for the gazillionth time.

Nothing happens.

The stone's broken.

Or she's broken. Or she will be, very soon. Each breath is starting to hurt. Her skin feels like it's slowly roasting. And she can barely see anymore.

And the two men—Skins—closing in on her have her death already planned out. She can see it in their eyes.

"Ada!" Tristan calls out again.

But she doesn't answer. What's the point?

She tries to send out a bolt of electricity, but her energy supplies dried up minutes ago. She dispatched three of them before her batteries ran empty.

She swallows, even though her mouth feels like the Sahara. This isn't supposed to happen. She should be in a shiny purple suit, blasting these bastards with everything she has.

Instead, she's cowering in a corner, flames licking at her

back and stinging her nostrils with the scent of burnt hair, and two men are stalking closer and closer.

And she never got to make this right with Eric. She's going to die with him believing all this was more important to her than him.

Tristan breaks away from the huddle of Zodiacs, running at the Skin nearest him. "Run toward me!" he shouts.

The Skin on her right realizes it's him Tristan is referring to and he spins around, confirming that Tristan is making like a battering ram and coming straight at him. He turns back to Ada and launches into motion, becoming a bullet himself.

He's going to try to reach Ada before Tristan reaches him.

Ada does the only thing she can: she runs, too. Straight at the Skin. There's fire behind her, to her immediate left and right. All she has are two Skins between her and the chance of freedom.

And this is what Tristan told her to do.

The Skin's eyes blaze almost as bright as the flames as he registers she's coming to him. Behind, Tristan's deep purple suit lifts off the ground. But even flying, he won't get to the Skin before the assassin reaches her.

Everything slows and speeds up at once. Ada can see the way the Skin's face glistens with sweat, the streaks of soot giving him a ghoulish look. The way the smile slowly dies as his face hardens.

And yet there's only a split second to execute her plan. The moment before she reaches the Skin, she twists. Turns. And runs at the second Skin.

She'd much rather face an unsuspecting murderer rather than one who's already planned out how to kill her.

She dives into a cloying cloud of smoke, coughing as tears run down her cheeks, preparing to fight when she comes out the other side.

She slams into a body and instantly starts hitting. Kicking. Throwing everything she has into surviving.

"Ada," says a soft voice.

A familiar voice.

A voice she recognizes at a soul level.

"Eric!"

She stills, her hands gripping the arms holding her. But although the shape of the body that faces her is familiar, it's encased in silver-blue metal. Eric's in his Aquarius suit.

It's the most beautiful thing she's ever seen.

The second Skin is writhing not far away, no doubt racked with pain.

"You knew," she whispers.

Eric knew she wouldn't run at the first Skin. That although the first was an imminent threat, that *because* the first was an imminent threat, she'd hedge her bets with the second. And he took him out before she even got here.

"Are you okay?"

It's Tristan's voice that has her spinning around. "Yes." Because Eric knew the way she thinks. Possibly even before she did.

Tristan startles when he sees Eric standing beside her. "Thank pitch you came back." He grabs Ada's hand and hauls her back to the others. "We need to get out of here."

Ada turns around to grab Eric, too, only to find thick acrid smoke. "Eric!"

But there's no sound beyond the roar of the fire, no movement beyond the dancing flames and the billows of smoke.

"Eric—"

Ada's scream is cut off by a mighty sound of tearing timber. Tristan pulls her in close as another section of ceiling falls, this time a massive beam. The Zodiacs beneath it scatter, but Jareth's only taken a step when the beam lands on him. He collapses, the heavy weight landing on his chest.

"Jareth!" Brielle screams as she rushes back.

"I'm fine," he groans. "Just get this off me."

"Stand back," Tristan tells Ada.

The four Zodiacs quickly move around Jareth, each finding a section of beam to grip, uncaring of the flames licking its surface. They're about to lift when a Skin knocks Brielle out of the way. She tumbles to the ground, but Tristan has dispatched the Skin with a furious volley of punches.

More Skins move in, recognizing that one Zodiac is down, and the others are distracted trying to save him. This is the break they needed.

Ada's heart thunders in her chest as she watches helplessly. There's nothing she can do to help. To prevent the butchering that's about to happen.

So much for the Gemini soulmates being the power to end all this.

She gasps, smoke stinging her throat. She's not Tristan's soulmate. She can't be.

If she was, then she'd be in a purple suit right now. She never would've promised her heart to someone else. To Eric.

Ada quickly tucks the tanzanite in her pocket and grips her locket. The one she's owned as long as she's known Eric. *Please let this work...*

"Akash."

The locket pops open as if it hasn't been fused shut all her life. Inside sits a glistening green gem. Knowing there's no time to acknowledge what just happened, she holds it tightly and repeats the word.

"Akash."

This time, something happens. Something amazing. Ada's swallowed by liquid metal the color of the forest, and she welcomes it. The moment she's engulfed, she draws in a deep breath. Her lungs fill with clean air, her eyes no longer sting or stream endless tears.

An energy she's never known, and yet instantly recognizes, powers through her.

She looks around, her sharp gaze slicing through the smoke. Tristan is fighting the Skins, Brielle beside him as they try to hold the tide of evil back. Logan's attempting to lift the beam with Cassandra, but it's barely budging. A Skin breaks past and leaps onto Logan's back. He spins around and shoves him off, Jareth's back arching as the weight settles on him again.

It's time to do her part.

Ada clenches her hands, finding the energy within her, glorying in the way it now feels endless. Limitless. And completely in her control.

She throws her shoulders back, looks up at the blazing ceiling, and draws in every atom of energy in the room.

And she detonates.

Arcs of light spear from her hands, splitting and branching until countless bolts streak through the air like veins of light. Each one finds a target. The Skins.

They all convulse, some screaming, some gurgling, most of them silent as they drop to the floor. Electrocuted.

No longer a threat.

Tristan and Brielle rush to help Logan and Cassandra. Ada joins in as they all lift the burning beam off Jareth.

"Let's get out of here. Now!" shouts Tristan, and the sound reverberates through Ada's helmet. They can talk to each other in these things!

Tristan grabs her hand and leaps, and she finds herself launching into the air. They soar through the hole in the roof, through crimson flames and onyx smoke, finally finding a shred of sky. His hand firmly holding hers, he leads her as the others follow and they land in quadrangle behind the orphanage.

"Retract your suits. Quick," he says.

Ada hears the others murmur the words as she says it. In a blink, her suit is gone, and the heat of the burning building hits her. She blinks as ash stings her eyes. She turns to the others, still trying to understand what's going on.

Tristan looks just as shocked as she is. "You're the Virgo."

His words confirm what she already realized. She's not the Gemini Twin! Tristan isn't her soulmate.

She spins around, eyes scanning for Eric. Her true soulmate.

Jareth is there, Brielle, Cassandra, Logan, and Tristan. But no Eric.

Veronica appears, taking a wide berth around what's left of the blazing orphanage. "Jareth," she cries on a sob.

He opens his arms, and she falls into them. "You're okay?"

"It's quite the story, but yes, we all are. Ada saved us."

Because Eric saved her.

Ada gasps. "Eric! He could still be in there!"

Veronica frowns. "I just saw him. He was driving away."

Relief scorches through Ada. Eric's safe.

Immediately followed by a rush of anguish. And he just left. He doesn't know she's not the Gemini Twin.

There's a shout somewhere and Veronica steps back. "They're here!" she shouts. "I found them!"

As the firefighters swarm around them, Ada's world mutes. She vaguely hears one of the men ask Tristan if it was necessary for all of them to run in after the kid.

Her blurry eyes see Tristan shrug. "There's safety in numbers."

She's certainly surrounded by more people than she has been in a very long time. Their faces hold relieved smiles and burdened frowns as the orphanage steadily becomes a blazing skeleton.

Ada tries to breathe but finds it far harder than she should. She found where she belongs. She's a Zodiac.

And yet it's a hollow victory.

Because she belongs with Eric.

BRIELLE

The stench of stale smoke fills the air as the wreckage of Grace Orphanage becomes a circus of frightened orphans, frantic nuns, and frenzied firefighters and medics.

Brielle and the Zodiacs do everything they can to help. Tristan and Logan help cart the injured into ambulances. Jareth and Veronica help the nuns corral and calm the younger children as Cassandra tries to reassure the teens. And Brielle and Ada work together to soothe the infants, feeding them, rocking them, doing just about anything to pacify their cries.

Brielle is relieved that she doesn't have to face the older kids, especially with the way Marie keeps looking at her. Marie knows who she is. She'd promised to keep her secret, but for how long? Would the fact that Brielle saved her life undo the decade long grudge Marie has held against her?

She'd rather not think about it. Not with everything else going on.

Ada is shushing and bouncing a baby beside her.

She's not Tristan's Gemini soulmate. She's the Virgo Guardian. Brielle realizes that some part of her should feel relief. That she still has time to see that look in his eyes for a little bit longer.

But she's not relieved. When she thought Ada was the missing Gemini, it was devastating. And now knowing that Ada isn't doesn't reseal the wound in her heart. Because she knows that Tristan finding his match is inevitable.

As she rocks the wailing infant in her arms, she wonders, is this how it's going to be every time they find a new Zodiac? Is she going to be crushed into smaller and less recognizable pieces of herself until there's nothing left? She doesn't want to postpone the pain any longer. She'd really rather just rip the band-aid off and be done with it.

For the first time since she met Tristan, she hopes he does find his twin, and as soon as possible. The sooner it happens, the sooner she can move on.

The sound of her phone ringing startles the babe that had finally started to quiet, sending him into a fresh wave of cries, so she fumbles to quickly answer the call.

It's Kerrim—she had hoped it was Bea with news of Frank.

"Hi," she answers in a small voice.

"Hey, is everything okay?" His voice wavers with uncertainty. "I hate that I had to leave you like that. I wanted to make sure you were safe."

She floats in silence for a moment, not sure how to answer. Physically, yes, she's okay. Emotionally? Mentally? Spiritually? Absolutely not.

"I'm not hurt," she replies. "We managed to get most out before the first responders arrived."

"Most?" he asks, and she wishes he hadn't.

"Yes, one of the nuns"—her voice cracks—"didn't make it..." A tear drops onto the baby's already wet cheeks.

He makes a small groan. "Oh no, I'm so sorry. I can meet up with you later tonight if you want. Anything you need."

What she needs he can't give her. For Sister Agatha to be still here. For Frank not to be in prison. For her heart not to be a shredded mess of what it used to be.

"No, it's fine," she dismisses. "I just need to rest." And to be alone.

He sighs, and she can imagine him nodding his head. "Okay, well, I'm just a call away if you need me."

"Thanks." She hangs up and slips the phone back into her pocket to return her full attention to the baby she's cradling.

But as she looks up, she sees paramedics carting a black body bag down the sidewalk to the coroner's van, and it's suddenly all she can focus on.

Time slows as she watches the men pull the stretcher off the curb, open the back doors, and transfer the bag into the van. Her soul wails so loudly it rivals the baby's cries. Brielle wants to run to the van, to throw herself into it and wrap herself tightly around Sister Agatha and never let go. But she's frozen in place, staring helplessly as the woman who raised her is carted away forever.

The men close the doors, and the gentle touch of a warm hand landing on her shoulder shakes her out of her paralysis.

She doesn't need to turn her head to know it's Tristan. She'd know his touch even if she were blind and deaf.

"I'm so sorry." His words, though soft, are weighted, as if they're not just apologizing for what happened here tonight.

She doesn't look at him. She can't, otherwise she'll break down.

"I know how much you loved her."

Brielle nods slowly.

His fingers lightly knead the mound of her shoulder. "I'm here for you, whatever you need."

She shakes her head, unable to stop herself. "But for how long?"

His hand freezes on her shoulder. "What do you mean?"

Finally, she turns to him and meets his confused, stricken gaze, stepping away until his hand falls off. "We can't keep doing this, Tristan."

He bites his lip and closes his eyes as if they burn. Then he shakes his head. "Ada isn't the Gemini. I don't know what went wrong during the test—maybe her electricity sparked the gem and made it look like it glowed. But the suit wouldn't respond. She can't be the Gemini."

Brielle bites back a sob. "No, but some day, somebody will be. And I can't keep hoping that the next Zodiac won't be her. I can't keep letting myself fall back in love with you every time they aren't."

"What are you saying?" His face is contorted, and she could almost swear Eric is here using his powers on him.

A frustrated sigh quakes its way out of her. "I don't know. But for now, I just need you to leave me alone."

He looks at her for a long moment, and she has to literally bite her tongue to keep from taking it back, from rushing to put her arms around him and remove the pain from his eyes.

At long last, he steps back and raises his hands in surrender. "Okay," is all he says before walking away.

Maybe this time, for good.

ADA

Ada wheels her chair from the computer she was sitting at to the next one, the sound loud in the darkened HQ. She types rapidly, brows pinched in focus.

It's been a week, and still no sign of Eric.

It was his disappearance that had her searching every room in the lower floor beneath Tristan's house. Her house, technically.

Except she'll never be able to call it home, not until Eric's back by her side.

Which is why this has to work.

It. Has. To.

She wheels to the next computer and types again. She couldn't believe her luck when she found the metal briefcase tucked in one of the last rooms. She'd opened it, gasping at the treasure it held.

Technology.

Alien technology.

Alien technology that makes everything she's been doing look like high school computer science.

She's spent every waking moment installing it

exploring it, and bringing it online. Every minute she'd worked had been a prayer. A plea. A desperate bid to find Eric.

"Ada?"

She leaps, spinning around with her hand outstretched, energy already crackling between her fingers.

Tristan raises a brow as he stops in the doorway of HQ. "I'm glad you have your powers under control," he says wryly.

Ada sags as the adrenaline disperses as quickly as it spiked. "It's amazing what a girl can do with the right stone."

Tristan enters, and she notes his chest is bare apart from the towel slung over his shoulders. He lifts up a corner to wipe the sweat from his face, not seeming to notice his tracksuit pants are slung low on his hips. He sighs. "If only we'd known you didn't have control of your powers when you made the tanzanite glow."

Ada turns back to the computer, grief heavy in her heart. "There were a lot of things we didn't know."

She rushed into this, hadn't slowed down to consider who she'd hurt if she didn't. And it was Eric who paid the price.

Tristan comes to stand beside her. "What are you still doing up?"

She glances at him, making a point of noting he's obviously just come from the gym. "I could ask you the same thing. It's one o'clock in the morning and you're doing a workout?" She arches her own brow. "The six pack couldn't wait?"

Her gaze travels over his lean physique. Tristan's definitely hot and hunky, all lithe grace and masculine beauty. She's sure his Gemini Twin will be happy with the package; how could she not be?

But his ridges and planes don't stir anything in her

beyond appreciation for any beautiful body. He's someone else's hot and hunky.

And her soul has its own mate.

Tristan shrugs. "I couldn't sleep."

She sighs. "Me neither." She wheels to the next computer. "Especially when I'm almost done."

"So, you're actually going to tell me what you've been doing?"

For the first time since the fire that destroyed the orphanage and her soul deep connection to Eric, Ada allows herself a spark of hope. She zooms back to the first computer, projecting it onto the largest screen on the wall. "Wait till you see it," she says, the excitement bubbling up against her will.

Tristan narrows his eyes at the screen, trying to make sense of the numbers and letters scrolling across it. "You could be hacking into Nebula again and I wouldn't be able to tell."

"There's no need," she says smugly. "The briefcase that I found. The technology in there..." Ada throws her hands out, trying to encompass exactly how endless the capabilities are. "We're talking connection to any satellite we want, including ones outside our galaxy if we find them. A way to know if anything unusual is happening around this house for a four-mile radius."

Tristan's eyebrows shoot up. "Four miles?"

"Yep. Skins won't be sneaking up on us." She drops her chin. "Because we now have dark matter detectors."

This time, Tristan's eyes pop wide open. "No way."

"Yes way," she shoots back. She spins around, typing even faster now. "But all this means there will be a lot of data to be scanned and processed. From here, from around the world, from space. We can't afford to miss anything."

Like Eric's location.

Tristan moves closer, his gaze sharp. "What do we need to do? Coordinate shifts between all the Zodiacs? Do you need more hardware? Software?"

Ada grins. "What do you know about artificial intelligence?"

"Ah, like robots who can talk and stuff?"

"Essentially." She turns back to the keyboard and taps the execution code, her stomach tightening. "But when you add alien technology, you get a little more than that."

The large screen flickers and turns black. Ada's tempted to hold her breath, but she knows this will take a few minutes. Instead, she fills the air with information. "AI enables computers to learn and interpret patterns, leverage programmed knowledge to offer advice or make decisions, all while extracting and analyzing language algorithms. Pretty cool, huh?"

"I get the feeling the answer is yes," Tristan says dryly. "If you could talk in English, then maybe I'll be able to keep up."

"Essentially, AI can do everything we need it to do. "But," Ada grins again, this time even wider. "If one adds a sprinkling of alien technology, then you get—"

The screen flashes as hundreds of blue pixels pour into the center. Tristan's eyes narrow as he watches. Ada pushes to her feet, her heart thumping. They're about to find out whether her week of late nights and early mornings have paid off.

The pixels swirl, forming lines then curves. They start to consolidate in some areas, fanning out in others as they create hills and valleys, light and shadow. Within seconds, they've undeniably created the three-dimensional image of a female face.

Ada claps her hands to her chest, her throat feeling tight. "Tristan, I'd like you to meet Esther."

Tristan looks at Ada, his face moving from baffled to

bewildered and back again.

"Hello, Tristan," comes a soft maternal voice from the room's speakers.

Tristan stands stock still, his jaw slightly slack. "Ah, nice to meet you, Esther."

"Your body temperature is falling, Tristan. I'd recommend putting on a shirt."

Ada snorts out a laugh as he shakes his head. "I can see who programmed you, Esther."

"Thank you, Tristan."

He turns to Ada. "Impressive. So she'll be doing all the scanning and processing, huh?"

She nods. "I suspect what Esther can do is going to blow even my mind."

Bringing Esther to life is something beyond her wildest dreams, whatever comes next isn't limited by the realms of possibility.

"Your energy levels are low, Ada," her computer states matter of factly. "Rest is required."

It's Tristan's turn to snort. It seems Esther is going to be a maternal figure in their life. And a bossy one at that.

Ada opens her mouth to respond, but a wave of tiredness washes over her, dragging at her muscles. Her shoulders sag. Esther's right. She's exhausted. The hours upon hours it took to bring Esther to life suddenly feel like boulders, steadily crashing down on her.

And now that Esther is live, she can rest. An advanced artificial intelligence system is going to be scanning for any signs of changes in dark matter. The moment Eric uses his powers, she'll be able to pinpoint his location.

"You're right," she says on a sigh. "I'm going to bed."

Tristan frowns. "We'll find him, Ada," he promises. "We'll make this right."

She nods, even though her head now feels too heavy to do

even that. "That's the plan."

They turn to leave HQ, and Tristan wraps his arm around her shoulder. She leans in, naked chest and all. Although they're not soulmates, there's a deep connection between all the Zodiacs. It's what makes them family.

She has to believe it's what will bring Eric back to her.

They've just reached the doorway when Esther's voice reaches them. "Ada. Tristan."

"Yes, Esther?" she asks tiredly as they separate and turn around.

"I'm detecting changes in the wormhole. It's expanding."

Tristan stills. "Expanding?"

"Yes, expand: to increase in extent, size, volume, or scope."

His lips twist. "Thanks."

"You're welcome. In this case, the event horizon surrounding the black hole is steadily increasing."

Ada clutches her locket. She didn't expect for something like this to happen. And not so soon. "What do you advise, Esther?"

"Processing level of risk," she responds calmly.

Ada and Tristan look at each other. She wonders if his gut is churning just like hers.

"Taking into account an extremely high probability of this being an unwanted development, and the likelihood of severe consequences, I have one recommendation."

Ada holds her breath and she's pretty sure Tristan's doing the same. That muscled chest of his isn't moving.

"Find out what's on the other side before it arrives."

Ready for the next installment in the Zodiac Guardians series? Check out AQUARIUS UNDONE!

AQUARIUS UNDONE

Twelve teens. One task.
Save the Universe.

Believing he's lost everything, Eric's decided to disappear. He's determined to never be vulnerable again, living with the irony that he can alleviate everyone's pain but his own.

Except he can't deny his draw to Ada and the others. And Ada is desperately trying to make things right between them. What's more, the Zodiacs are quickly learning they were connected long before any of them realized.

And the Zodiacs need him. The wormhole is changing. It's growing bigger and Tristan has had another vision. A planet is about to be destroyed, and they're the only ones who can stop the destruction from happening.

Eric, his heart jaded and guarded, learns it's his own home world in danger, the Aquarius planet. Ada wants to be there for him, if only he'd let her in...

Can the Zodiacs save Aquarius and its people? Or are they walking straight into Chardis's trap?

Grab your copy HERE!

mybook.to/AquariusUndone

MORE EPIC ROMANCE TO FALL IN LOVE WITH!

ALSO BY TAMAR SLOAN

PRIME PROPHECY SERIES

KEEPERS OF THE GRAIL

KEEPERS OF THE CHALICE

KEEPERS OF THE LIGHT

KEEPERS OF EXCALIBUR

DESTINED DEMIGODS

ELEMENTAL GAMES

THE SOVEREIGN CODE

THE THAW CHRONICLES

ALSO BY TRICIA BARR

THE MATING GAMES

THE BOUND ONE SERIES

THE AMARANT SERIES

SHIFTER ACADEMY

HEAVENLY SINNERS

ABOUT THE AUTHORS

By day, Tricia is a full time mom to two beautiful girls and a wife/business partner to a handsome hard-working husband. By night—and nap times—she's a USA Today Best-selling Author of unique and thrilling teen and adult fantasies inspired by her vivid, somewhat creepy dreams and her own adventures around the world.

Tamar hasn't decided whether she's a psychologist who loves writing, or a writer with a lifelong fascination with psychology. She must've been someone pretty awesome in a previous life (past life regression indicates a Care Bear), because she gets to do both. When not reading, writing, or working with teens, Tamar can be found with her husband and two sons enjoying country life in their small slice of the Australian bush.